UNLAWFUL RESTRAINT

The Hidden Survivor Book 2

CONNOR MCCOY

CHAPTER ONE

ALTHOUGH STILL FRUSTRATED by his captivity and the unre-solved incident with Anna, Glen was feeling just a little smug. During a stop at the bathroom on his trip back from the house, he was able to remove a broom handle from the part that does the sweeping and smuggle it into the closet. Bossman wasn't paying that much attention to him anymore. He didn't even notice that Glen had stuffed a broom handle down the leg of his pants and the rest was sticking up, tucked under his arm.

They'd dragged a mattress into his closet while he was tending to Anna. Glen slid the broom handle along the far edge of the mattress, where it couldn't be seen by a person standing in the doorway. He wasn't sure what he was planning on doing with it, but he was sure it would come in handy. If nothing else, he could use it as a weapon and get out of this place.

He wasn't sure if the darkness was a blessing or a curse. On one hand, the constant light deprivation was affecting his mood, on the other, he was pretty sure he'd be bored out of his mind in this closet with nothing to do if he did have a light. He was floating in the darkness in a kind of half sleep. He couldn't tell if his eyes were open or closed. He listened to the sounds coming from within the house, trying to understand the rhythm of the place and how many people lived there.

His thoughts drifted to Sara and how utterly mesmerizing she was at Mia and Sally's age. She'd been so independent and not at all impressed by the fact he had been in med school. He was a resident in neurology and, so, very full of himself. She brought him down to size with one yawn.

He'd been trying to impress her with his credentials. Talking about his prospects, his career path. He'd just finished recounting a tricky surgery he'd undertaken and how well the patient was doing when she yawned.

She apologized immediately, stating late nights and a heavy course load, but he'd never really gotten over her reaction. It was as though she was saying 'I'm the important one here, and don't you forget it.' He'd realized that he'd been monopolizing the conversation, that he knew next to nothing about her and wouldn't if he didn't start asking questions.

She'd been brilliant. The moon to his moth. The next time he'd run into her had been at a party. He'd been bragging to his friends about his prospects when he noticed she was nearby. He kept bragging and caught her eye, flashing her a smile. She'd raised one eyebrow at him and turned away.

He hadn't seen her again that evening, or any evening afterward for a long time.

They might not ever have gotten together except he was on a panel of doctors talking about neurological disorders and their treatments. By that time he'd begun pioneering a cure for a rare genetic brain disorder and had lectured at length about the benefits of the procedure. Sara had been in the audience. She'd liked the serious Glen much more than the posturing Glen and had asked if they could get coffee and talk about the physiology of brains. He'd agreed, of course.

And he'd wised up. He stopped talking about himself and instead talked about things he knew. Sara was interested in the anatomy of the brain and how it functioned, wanted to know what was known and unknown. She wanted to know what emotions really were and where depression came from and was studying the logic-emotion connection and why some people acted on feelings even when they knew the result would be detrimental.

They'd continued meeting and talking throughout that year, and finally, she agreed to go on a date where they would do fun things and not talk about the brain at all. She was so smart and funny, and he couldn't help falling in love with her. But she gave up so much when she married him. And he regretted that now.

If he could bring her back, he'd do a lot of things differently, as the Kenny Chesney song says. They would find a way for her to keep doing the work she loved. They could have hired someone to take care of the house, and Clarence too, when he was born. It had been so unfair of him to make her quit her job, so egotistical. He was ashamed of himself.

But he was trying to make it up to her now, taking care of Christian, Mia, and Sally. He hoped Mia had been able to get Christian the anti-biotics. It weighed on his mind. If she hadn't, then Christian would be dead now. But then they all could be gone. Terror's men could have tracked them down. He wouldn't be surprised if Terror had outsiders executed.

He'd been confused about Terror. He'd seemed almost decent until he'd smacked Glen on the head. And then there was Anna. Terror had shown no emotion about the state of that girl. If she'd been in Glen's care, he would have been livid about her physical and emotional state. He would have hunted the man who'd abused her and made him pay.

It seemed likely to Glen that Terror was the perpetrator of the violence. He'd battered that girl and possibly raped her too. It may have started out consensual, but the minute his fist had inflicted that damage it had become rape. What was Glen going to do about that? What could he do? He didn't have much power here. Maybe none at all. He only was needed when the community's doctor was drunk, it seemed.

Glen wondered if Terror was psychotic. He showed signs of psychosis. That Terror was quick to anger, showed a lack of empathy, and displayed a certain amount of grandiosity was clear. Perhaps he'd hit his head growing up. Maybe there was an actual physical reason for Terror's behavior. Glen would like to get a look inside Terror's brain. A lot could be explained by a quick look-see.

He'd become so used to floating in and out of consciousness that when the noise woke him he wasn't sure if he'd dreamt it. But it came again shortly, the pop, pop, pop of gunfire. It wasn't close, probably at the border of the town. Was it Christian, Mia, and Sally? Had his trio discovered weapons and come to rescue him? Or maybe they weren't here to save him, but to plunder the town. They had admitted that they were prepared to kill people.

He got up and felt his way to the door, testing the handle to see if it still was locked, even though he'd already tried it. Damn those kids. They didn't know what they were up against. If Terror got hold of the girls, who know what he'd do. He'd lay good money on the chances that Anna's injuries were at Terror's hand. The man was unstable. Maybe even psychotic.

The gunshots continued ringing out, and he thought maybe they were coming closer? It was hard to tell from in here. How long could the three of them hold out against a town full of gun-toting men?

Then the screaming and crying started nearby. And so

many guns. Too many for it to be Glen's trio. And probably there were things going on out there that he didn't want to see. But he was a sitting duck in this closet. Nowhere to escape the bullets when they found him. He felt his way back to the mattress and grabbed the broom handle. He almost tripped moving back to the door but caught himself.

Shoving the broom handle in the crack of the door, Glen pushed with all his weight, trying to pry the door open. Nothing. The door wouldn't budge. And suddenly the wood cracked and Glen's head slammed against the wall. There was a sharp pain, and stars flashed in front of his eyes. The damn broom handle had broken.

He considered if he should pound on the door. The drawbacks were evident. If the wrong person heard him and opened the door, he could be dead. And he didn't know who the wrong persons were. Would the group overtaking the town free him because he was a prisoner of the original inhabitants, or would they consider him one of them and just shoot him? That's what Terror would do, he thought. Why bother to deal with the unknown? Just kill him and get it over with.

Glen banged his head gently against the door. What should he do? Hide in the corner behind the mattress? Pretend to be dead? Maybe it didn't matter. Perhaps they wouldn't bother to open this door, and he would die of dehydration. No one knew he was here, and no one ever would.

He shook the negative thoughts from his head. There was no time for morbidity. He had to think his way out of this closet before he was at the mercy of whoever found him here. He tried pressure on the handle in different degrees and at different angles, but it was no use. The door wouldn't budge.

He went back to sit on his mattress, what remained of the broom handle across his lap. He wished there was at least a little light because he knew he would be blinded if the door

did open. There was gunfire all around now, yelling, screaming, and sobbing. His nerves were on edge. So far nothing
seemed to be affecting this house. No bullets were thudding
into the woodwork. No screaming or yelling or crying from
within.

How much longer would that last? He felt fear building
inside him, and he shook his head. There were probably a
hundred houses in this town, many of them would be
untouched by whatever the hell was going on out in the
streets. He probably was safe until the fighting stopped
anyway. He should try resting until the fighting came to him.

CHAPTER TWO

MIA WAS SLOGGING along in the rain at the back of the pack. Her cheek was stinging again, but at least Sally was paying attention now, and she'd stopped letting branches whip back and smack Mia. The rain was pounding, and she hoped they would get there soon. She would love to be dry and warm. Christian was leading them deftly through the woods. He'd apparently memorized the way, because he forged on confidently, not needing to stop and consider which direction they were going. He knew.

Mia hoped it wouldn't take too long to get there. Her face was hurting, burning really, and she wanted to lie down and sleep for a really long time. It was probably the whole reaction to the medicine and then the effects of the epi-pen that had worn her out. It was all she could do to keep putting one foot in front of the other.

"Yes!" Christian exclaimed from in front of Sally. She hoped that meant they were nearing the house. Sure enough, he motioned them to slow down and creep along, and before long they popped out of the woods into the backyard of an old farmhouse.

Christian motioned them to stay behind a shed while he checked the house. Time seemed to crawl by. Mia sat on the grass and leaned back against the rough wood of the shed. It was wet from the rain, but she didn't care. She was tired.

She must have dozed off because the next thing she knew Sally was shaking her awake. "Come on," Sally said. "Christian just gave the all clear."

Mia got up and stumbled toward the farmhouse, where she hoped there might be an actual bed.

It was even better than that. Not only was there furniture but the propane tank still had fuel in it, and Christian was able to turn on the oven for heat.

"We could start a fire in the woodstove," Christian said, "but then someone might spot the smoke from the chimney. This way we can dry out without advertising to the world that we are here."

Mia pulled off her boots, jacket, and soggy sweater and hung them over the back of a chair to dry. Then she padded through the house in her socks looking for a place to lie down. Her damp feet left footprints on the dusty floor as she traveled from room to room. Whoever had left this house had cared for it. The furniture was covered in dust sheets, and there were rodent traps in strategic places. The mice had long since perished, and there was nothing left but little mouse skeletons.

She found a bedroom and pulled the sheet off the bed to reveal a brass bed frame and a mattress covered with a quilt. Mia pulled back the covers and saw a sandwich of blankets and clean sheets. There were no signs of mice, which surprised her. Surely the rodents would want bits of this to take back to their nests? Then she noticed the strange cones on the legs of the bed frame, kind of like the contraptions her grandma used to use to keep the squirrels out of her birdfeeder.

Somebody thought they'd be coming home.

She slipped out of her wet pants and pulled her T-shirt over her head, then she slid between the sheets and pulled the covers up around her neck. It had been so long since she'd slept in a bed that she couldn't remember where it had been. It felt like heaven. She rolled onto her side and went to sleep.

She woke to the sound of distant gunfire.

She rummaged in the closet and pulled out an old jacket and put it on. Then she picked up her damp clothes and carried them back into the kitchen. The room had been turned into a laundry room. The wet clothes from their packs had been draped over every available surface, and Christian and Sally had even run a line across the length of the room.

It may have looked like a laundry room, but it smelled like heaven. Something was bubbling in the pot on the stove. She lifted the lid and inhaled the fragrance of chicken soup and rice. It was thick and hot, and her mouth was watering like crazy. Hopefully, they could eat soon.

Mia tossed her pants and T-shirt over the line and went in search of the others. She found them in the pantry, listening at the window. Mia was distracted by the cans of food lined up on the shelves. They wouldn't have to forage again for ages.

"Where's the gunfire coming from?" she asked, and both Christian and Sally jumped and turned around. "Sorry," Mia said, "didn't mean to startle you."

"We think it's coming from the town," Christian said. "And we think we might be able to use it to our advantage."

"How's that?" Mia asked.

"We could sneak into the town under cover of the chaos," Sally said. "And then we could search for Glen."

"Wouldn't that be dangerous?" Mia asked. "It sounds pretty serious out there."

"We'd have to be careful to stay away from the battle,"

Christian said. "If the fighting is in the south we go in from the north. Or the other way around, depending."

"So, we sneak over the wall and do a house to house search?" Mia asked, but she didn't expect an answer. "That still sounds dangerous. We'll really have to blend in with the scenery."

"If we are on the opposite side of the town from the fighting, no one will be looking in our direction," Christian said.

Mia couldn't help but think otherwise. If it were her, she'd post guards all around the wall to prevent an ambush. They'd just have to be extremely careful.

"Can we eat first?" Mia asked. "I'm starving for some real food."

"We already ate," Sally said. "We're keeping it hot for you. Come on, I'll serve you."

They stepped back into the kitchen and Sally grabbed a bowl from the cupboard. She wiped it with a towel from a drawer.

"Dusty," she said, looking at Mia, "but the towels were stored in a plastic bag, so they are clean."

She filled the bowl using a giant metal ladle and took it into the dining room where a place setting already had been laid for Mia. When Christian sat at the table, Sally set a cup of something hot in front of him. Mia sat at the first real dining table that she'd seen in months. Sally disappeared from the room and came back with a large mug of tea and some of the travel bread. Mia waved the bread away.

"Right now, I feel as if I'll never willingly eat that stuff again," she said. She looked down in her bowl. "But this? This looks like paradise."

She dipped her spoon into the bowl and blew on the contents. The first bite was too hot, and she had to hold her hand over her mouth and pant until it was cool enough to swallow.

Christian laughed.

"I did that too," he said. "I was so hungry for a hot meal that I burned my tongue."

"Yeah, me too," Sally said sitting across from Christian. "I had to drink cold water because, of course, there isn't any ice. Need electricity for that."

Mia remembered her mother had said to eat the soup near the edge of the bowl because it cooled faster. So, she let the next spoonful cool a little longer before putting it in her mouth. That helped. She actually could taste the soup.

She closed her eyes as she swallowed, feeling the warmth spread through her. She would remember this meal for the rest of her life.

"Good, right?" Sally said. "I never in my life thought canned chicken and rice soup would taste so good. I ate way too much."

"Mmm," Mia responded. "So good. Orgasmic really."

"I wouldn't go that far," Christian said. "It is only soup."

"Best soup ever," Sally said.

Mia ate with delight as the others planned their attack on the town.

"You've been there, Mia," Christian said, "what do you think?"

"There are a lot of houses to search," Mia said. "And you know there are going to be families hiding in some of them. What are we going to do about those people?"

"That's a whole issue of its own," Sally agreed. "We can't kill them all."

"I don't want to kill any of them," Mia said. "That was always a stupid idea."

"Wasn't it your idea?" Christian asked raising his eyebrow.

"Might have been," Mia said. "But it was just a reaction to what was going on. If Glen taught me anything, it's that you have to hang on to your humanity. Remember your compassion."

"That's what we're doing, isn't it?" Christian asked. "Going to rescue him?"

"Yes. That's what we are doing." Sally gave Mia a look through half-closed eyes. "If someone ever finishes eating."

"I'm done." Mia jumped out of her chair. "I just need to get dressed."

They pulled on their driest clothes and then their raincoats. Sally went as far as rummaging through the drawers in the bedroom to find clean underwear and dry pants.

"Really?" Christian asked. "You are going to wear someone else's underwear?"

"How is that any different from eating off their plates?" Sally asked. "I'm tired of stinking to high heaven, and all of my clothes are still damp. I just want to be clean and dry."

Mia dropped the pistol into her raincoat pocket, and Christian hefted the shotgun. Two firearms weren't going to save them from an army, but they might come in useful against a single assailant.

They left the farmhouse by the rear door and scooted back into the forest at the back. They weren't going to use the front of the house at all, because if it continued to look disused then maybe no one would bother them. Mia hoped that was the case, anyway. She was happy to stay there as long as possible. It was better than trespassing on Glen's hospitality. And it had enough bedrooms for all them. To say nothing of enough food.

She put a hand on her full belly. Never had food satisfied her more. The freshwater mussels had been okay, but they weren't really her thing. They hadn't really filled her up like the soup had. It was so thick they could have called it stew, as far as she was concerned. That was probably because Sally had added so much extra rice and then a can of chicken broth. She'd asked Sally about it while they'd been getting dressed.

They found an unused path in the woods that headed in what seemed like the right direction and followed it. It was clear no one had been on it for a while. Branches were growing across it and clumps of leaves were scattered along it. But it still was easier than hacking their way through the forest. And not nearly as exhausting.

Rain dripped on them from the trees and through the trees and Mia's pant legs soon were as wet as they had been when they had reached the farmhouse. Her feet squelched in her sneakers. She really needed to find a pair of boots, but the worst part was the pain in her cheek. She hoped the scratch wasn't getting infected. She didn't dare take another shot of any kind of painkiller. Not after what had happened before.

She wondered what had happened to the over-the-counter drugs she thought she'd grabbed in the pharmacy. Maybe Glen had them? But they hadn't been in the bags when she'd joined up with Sally and Christian. Had they had fallen out? She would have given anything to have something that would ease the sting and the ache. She'd ignored it while she was eating because, well, because, duh, food.

Mia sniffed and wiped her nose with the back of her hand. The dampness was making it run, and she wished she was back in the dry farmhouse and there had been no gunshots and that Glen was with them, so they wouldn't have to investigate. She was glad she had Sally and Christian, and Glen, of course, but sometimes she wished they could just stay put and pretend to be normal for a while. Wouldn't that be nice?

Maybe they could now. There was plenty of food at the farmhouse, and if they just could keep from being discovered, they could stay there a while. She wondered what had happened to the people who had lived there, and why they had left a house so full of good stuff. Maybe they were living in the town now? Were they off somewhere hoping to come home to a house full of supplies? If that were the case, they'd be disappointed to find someone had been in their stuff. Like Goldilocks and the Three Bears.

Most likely, of course, they were dead. Something dreadful had happened to them and they never were coming back to the house. Mia was sorry if that was the case, but it certainly made it easier on her conscience to think they were gone. She didn't really like the dog-eat-dog nature of current society. She especially didn't like being one of the dogs. If they only had a house of their own.

Sally stumbled just ahead of Mia, reaching out to catch her arm so she wouldn't fall. Sally smiled at her wanly. She was tired, Mia thought. She should have slept instead of setting up the laundry and cooking food. They both should have rested, because now they were likely to make mistakes. Mia would have to keep an eye out for that. And when they got back, she'd offer Sally a turn in the big bed.

The gunshots had not abated and, in fact, had increased until it sounded like a battle. There was screaming now too. Mia wondered how close they were and if they should do a reconnaissance run so they didn't stumble into the fighting by accident.

"Christian," she said quietly, "wait up." She jogged past Sally at a wide spot in the trail and caught Christian's arm. "We should try seeing what's going on," she said. "So we don't run right into the fighting by mistake."

"How do you propose we do that?" he asked.

"One of us could sneak to the edge of the forest, or climb a tree and see what we can see?" Mia said, making it a question, so she didn't seem like she was taking over.

"I don't want to climb a tree," Christian said and turned to Sally. "Do you want to climb a tree?"

Sally shook her head wearily. She shouldn't be climbing any trees.

"I'll go," Mia said, looking around for a likely candidate. There was a big tree growing next to a large boulder. Mia thought if she could climb the boulder she'd be able to get into the tree's branches. She touched Christian's arm. "Can you help me get up there?" she asked.

Christian handed the shotgun to Sally and made a stirrup with his hands. She put her soggy sneaker into his hands. He grimaced but held still. "I suppose it would be too much to ask for a clean, dry shoe in my hands?" he said.

She smiled at him and said "One! Two! Three! Go!" She jumped as he boosted her up. She was just able to climb on top of the boulder, with a little scrabbling.

Mia stood up and looked around. The boulder was pretty tall, but not tall enough to top the forest by a long shot, so she reached for a branch and hauled herself up. She didn't know what kind of tree it was, but it was suitable for climbing. It had sturdy limbs that weren't too far apart, and they didn't start to get smaller until she was quite a way up. Finally, her head poked through the canopy, and she was able to see around her.

She wiped the rain from her face and saw they'd been traveling in the right direction, although she really already knew that because the noise had been getting louder. Whereas behind her there were trees and more trees, in front of her she could see the valley, the road, and the town. It looked as though the fighting was concentrated at the far end, which was good. They wouldn't have to skirt the settlement before they went in. However, there were sentries posted at the near edge as well, although they seemed to be paying more attention to the fighting at the other end of the town than to any threat coming from this direction. It was human nature, she thought, to keep an eye on the known risk, rather than look for something that may never materialize.

That would work in their favor, she decided, looking to see where they might cross the open land between forest and town without being seen. It was good that the three of them were covered in mud, their dirt would blend in with the wet world and make them less visible.

The library where she and Glen had been held was on this end of town, Mia noticed. So, they probably should look there first. After that, anyone's guess was as good as hers. She spent a few more minutes just watching, taking in details that might help them when they got there. Then she started back down the tree. She made it to the boulder without incident, but then was stymied about to how to get down.

She couldn't just jump, it was too far, and she couldn't drop from a tree branch for the same reason. What was she going to do?

"Christian," she hissed, "how do I get down from here? We didn't bring any rope."

Christian looked worried. He walked as far around the boulder as he could before the undergrowth got to be too much, and stepped back. He looked up to her. "You'll have to jump, and I'll catch you," he said.

"I'll crush you," she said.

"You're not that heavy," he said.

"I'll hurt you then." She looked around. "Why isn't there a convenient vine or something? There would be in Tarzan or Dr. Who."

"Why don't we zip our raincoats together? You can sling them over that branch and let yourself down that way." Sally asked. "Then Christian can catch you, and you won't bowl him over."

"You'll get wet," Mia said.

"Like we aren't wet already," Sally said, rolling her eyes.

"Come on, Christian, let's get this over with." She unzipped her raincoat, took Christian's and zipped them together.

She flung them upward, and on the third try, Mia was able to catch them. She took off her own jacket and zipped it to Sally's. She considered tying a sleeve to the branch, but if she did that they might not be able to get the coats back. And no one wanted to be running around in the rain with bullets flying without their raincoat on.

She settled for draping the coats over the branch and taking hold of both sides. She swung out and went into a partially controlled slide that felt entirely uncontrolled to her. She dropped and landed in Christian's outstretched arms, knocking him over and completely flattening him.

She rolled off him and couldn't contain her nervous laughter. He started laughing as well, and before she knew it, all three of them were laughing uncontrollably.

CHAPTER THREE

TERROR PACED the big entrance hall of the library. He thought about examining the maps on the big table in his favorite room, but his mood would ruin the place for him. Maybe forever. Why are they under attack again? Didn't he give these people the opportunity to stay? Didn't he offer protection? Food? Medicine? And they'd stabbed him in the back.

He needed this skirmish to be over so he could concentrate on finding the traitor who had raped the girl. Or at least hit the girl. That was unacceptable behavior, and he would punish the man who did it. He would beat him to within an inch of his life and then cut off his balls.

A voice in his head whispered that it would be difficult to cut off his own balls. He stopped a moment, puzzled. He had no memory of beating a girl, it couldn't have been him. "Oh, but it was," mocked the voice. "You and only you. No one else would dare do anything so brutal with you around to cut off their balls."

He stopped pacing and laid his face against the cold marble, a column at the far end of the hall. It felt so peaceful just to stand there, to become one with the stone. The voice in his head was wrong. He had not hurt the girl. She'd come to his bed willingly, and someone else had hurt her. That's what had happened and to hell with the voice in his head.

It was laughing now. Laughing at him, mocking him. He stood up and drove his fist into the pillar, breaking his knuckles.

When Angelica found him, he was sitting on the floor, his back against the cold marble column. He saw her coming toward him and wondered what she was worried about. Had something happened? He wanted to get up and meet her half-way, but really, it was too much trouble when he was so tired.

"What have you done to yourself?" she asked. "Your poor hand is mangled."

It was. The bones were broken, and blood was seeping from cuts and scrapes, even though it had been ages since he'd hit the column. At least it felt like ages. He didn't remember why he'd done it. What practical purpose could hitting a marble pillar serve?

"What happened?" she asked. "Did you get in a fight with someone?"

"Just this pillar," he said. "It insulted me." He gave her a weak smile.

She frowned at him, her eyes showing a look of concern. "Okay, well, let's get you up and get this taken care of." She took hold of his elbow and helped him to his feet.

"The doctor is drunk," he pointed out. "There's no point in trying to get him to fix this. It'll heal anyway." He looked at his hand and wondered if that were true. It was so purple and swollen it was hard to imagine it ever looking normal again.

"What about the other doctor?" she asked. "The one you have locked in a closet? He could take care of this."

"He's too close to the fighting," he said. "It would be too difficult to get him out of there."

"Then let me clean it up and wrap it until the gunfire lets up. Then I'll go get him. All we have to do is turn off the batteries, the lights will go out, and they won't be able to see to shoot. Come next door, I've got some supplies."

She led him out of the library and into the street. He pulled himself together and walked purposefully beside her. He was the leader in this town. What usually came so naturally took a lot of effort. He was grateful when Angelica pointed to the dining room table and told him to sit.

He sat with his eyes closed, felling his hand throb with every heartbeat. He wished he'd been smart enough to not hit a marble pillar. In his mind he rewrote the story. He'd engaged an intruder in hand-to-hand combat and, during the fray, he'd been slammed against the pillar, destroying his hand. Yes, that was it. He'd chased off an armed combatant with his bare hands.

"I see nothing amusing here," Angelica said. "What are you smiling at?"

He snapped his eyes open.

"I'm just planning what I'll do with those damn people from the settlement," he said. "I think it's time to burn it down. I should have chased them off a long time ago. I've got to overcome this damn sentimental streak. I never could stand to see a family evicted from their home."

"A sentimental streak? If you've got one, I've never seen it. I don't know what's going on in your head, but if it's as gory as that smile made me think, you'd better keep it away from the families here. Or you'll be losing more town folk. They're already spooked as it is."

She took a cloth and gently began washing his hand. He sucked in his breath as the soap stung his skin and the pressure sent jolts of pain through his fingers. When she was done washing, she dried it and wrapped it in gauze, giving him a mummy's hand. He cradled his hand against his body, trying to keep the pain off his face.

"Let's see if we can make it across town," she said. "I'd hate for people to think I let you get all gimpy on my watch."

"Why are you acting so nice?" he asked. "You aren't soft. You'd better not be humoring me. You know I despise that."

"I'm trying to get you to the doctor," she said. "You respond better to kindness than orders when you are hurt. If you are going to take out your frustration on me, then forget it. You can get yourself to the doctor."

"I don't need the doctor," he said. He felt the fire burning in his belly again, and he wanted to strike out at her, but he fought the urge. He needed to be presidential, not petty. "I'll heal just fine without a doctor."

"Sure, if you don't care if you are able to use your hand again. But if you want to be able to fire a gun, then you should get it seen to. You are not a stupid man, Tyrell, but sometimes you forget to use your brain."

"Many great leaders have injuries," Terror said. "It's how their followers recognize they've been victorious in battle. I won't need to shoot a gun if I have men to do it for me."

"Men and women," Angelica said.

"Of course, men and women. Why do you even need to say that? Have I ever discriminated against women? No."

"Look at the number of women compared to men," she said. "It's not exactly fifty-fifty."

"There aren't as many women with the skills I need as there are men," he said. "Or it would be fifty-fifty. Women are easier to work with, they don't get involved with all that macho one-on-one bull crap that men do."

"I don't think you are looking hard enough," she said. "I've worked with plenty badass women."

"You wouldn't catch a man coddling me," he said, ignoring her last point.

"I wouldn't catch any of your men within a hundred feet of you when you're injured. They stay far, far away. They are afraid of you, which may be smart, but it isn't very badass." She gave him a pointed look. "So, either get up off your ass and get a move on or don't. I'm tired of this conversation."

He glared at her. This was why he'd recruited her, of course. But he wasn't especially pleased that she wasn't afraid of him. Or, if she was scared, she knew how to keep it to herself. She was shorter than him by at least ten inches, and that was with her hair gelled up into spikes, but she wasn't intimidated by him. If it were possible, he'd even say she was bored by him in his current mood.

That she was bored rankled him. He considered himself many things, but boring was not one of them. Boring was dangerous. Men did not follow boring leaders. They followed men who inspired them. Men who had ideas, and knew how to bring them to fruition.

And hadn't he had visions that he'd brought to life? This town with lights and refrigeration powered by wind and solar energy, it was a monument to his know-how, his creativity, his balls. He was a ballsy leader. He knew how to get things done. If Angelica was bored with him, that was her problem. He was a dynamic and complex man.

He got up. "What are you waiting for?" he asked. "Let's get going."

CHAPTER FOUR

GLEN STOOD with his forehead against the door, listening to the sounds of battle outside. He could hear the cries of the wounded, but he couldn't get out of the damned closet to help. It wasn't until his legs started shaking that he realized he'd been standing there a very long time. He was hungry and thirsty, and no one had been to let him use the bathroom.

He found the broken broom handle and sat in the corner facing the door. Either no one would open that door ever again, in which case he would have to get creative about getting out of here, or someone would open the door. The problem was that someone who opened the door could be friend or foe, and he wouldn't know until the door opened, if even then.

He wondered if the hinges were on the inside or outside of the door. If the house was built correctly, they would be on the inside. But you never knew. And apparently the door had been modified so there were no cracks that outside light could stream through to illuminate the interior. If he were to take the time to do that, he'd damn well swap the hinges so his prisoner couldn't get out. Then again, they might not have thought about it.

He stood up to go to the door and swayed a little. He'd need food soon if he were to keep thinking clearly. He steadied himself against the wall and walked to the door. His fingers found the door jamb almost immediately, which he took as a good sign. He trailed his fingers across the wood to the frame on the other side and slid his fingers up the crack where door met frame.

He was in luck, his fingers caught the cold metal of the hinge where it protruded. He felt the pin that held the hinge together – the top of the bolt was flat, like a nail, but what would he find at the bottom?

Nothing. It was a straight pin. No screw, no nut, no plug at the bottom to keep him from removing the pin. Good. He wouldn't be clawing his way out through the walls after all. The second piece of good news that day.

He went back to his corner and waited. He wanted to think this through before he acted. Clearly, when it came to his captors, now would be a good time to escape. They were distracted by the invading force, whoever that was. But this might not be a fantastic time for attempting to flee the town. There were a lot of bullets flying around, and he doubted either side was clear on whose team he was on. Either side might shoot him.

Should he escape the room and then find another place to hide? Or just wait until the shooting stopped and see what had happened? He easily could wait until nightfall and sneak out later. That seemed the best course of action. He would wait until dark or, not knowing when night actually was, he'd wait until the town was silent. He'd be able to hear the clock chime. If it chimed twice and the place was quiet, then he'd sneak out.

He began to feel less shaky, surer of himself. He'd be able

to get food and water as soon as he let himself out of here, and that wouldn't be long now. He felt hope surge through his body, his heart beating intensely, his breathing firm. Terror had made a mistake and he, Glen, was going to take advantage of it. He smiled in the dark. He would enjoy getting the better of Terror, that was for sure.

The irony didn't escape him. He knew if he hadn't tried stealing from Terror, he wouldn't be in this predicament. But he also wasn't capable of letting the boy, Christian, die. He knew he was really a man, and not a boy, but he couldn't help noticing the similarities between Christian and Clarence, and Christian was a boy in need.

Of course, physically they were nothing the same. Christian was not yet three when he died. Clarence was a grown man. Christian had been a small boy, pale and thin-limbed. Clarence was a swarthy man, well-muscled and dark skinned, tattoos covering his arms and torso.

Wait.

He'd gotten their names confused. Clarence was his toddler son, Christian, the well-built man. How could he have switched them like that? They were melding in his brain, Christian was becoming Clarence to him. He supposed it was natural, in a way. Christian was vulnerable, hurt and dying. Glen could save him. If he rescued Christian, would it make up for not being able to help Clarence, his baby son who had expired in his arms?

His face was wet. He hadn't realized he'd been crying. He wiped his face with the hem of his Henley and pulled himself together. Sensory deprivation was unnerving him, sending him into a spiral of self-indulgent thoughts. He'd do better to concentrate on the task at hand.

He made himself listen to the conflict. Bullets thudding into wood and metal, the occasional scream or oath when they found flesh. The running feet. Voices calling "fall back," or "move in," and there were whispered voices in the house. There above him, murmurs and rustling, the cry of a child. He wasn't the only person trapped here.

There were boots on the porch steps, the front door was thrown open and crashed against the wall. Glen tensed himself, ready to fight, to defend himself the best he could. But the steps bypassed the room his closet was in. They went up another floor, and there was a hushed conversation. The voices of two women, he thought. Then a cracking sound he couldn't decipher and silence.

Nothing could be heard from above. No voices, no rustling, nothing. He began to fear the children had been killed and he was horrified. Even the most barbaric of people did not execute children. But that was before. Maybe now it was total annihilation for the losing side.

————

THE FIGHTING INCREASED as they headed toward the middle of town. Twice bullets ricocheted off the wall behind their heads before Terror let Angelica convince him to wait in the pharmacy while she scouted ahead. His hand was throbbing, and in the drug store, he could find painkillers while he waited for her to return. His head was pounding in time with his fist, and Terror needed a minute to collect himself. He seemed to be having trouble controlling his anger too, and that wasn't like him. He needed to calm down, to reset, or whatever it was that the New Age crystal gazers said.

"Stay put, so I can find you when I need to," she said as she left. He would have shot a man who dared to tell him what to do. But his knuckles stung and ached, so he waved her away with his other hand and turned to scan the products on the shelves.

He was surprised at how little there was. They would have

to raid another town. The odds and ends of products were a hodgepodge of things useful from the kitchen to the garage – if you had an imagination. There was a hot water bottle on one of the lower shelves, a helpful item, but not what he was looking for at the moment. When he didn't find anything but baby aspirin, he felt in his pocket for his keys and let himself into the medicine storage area behind the pharmacy counter.

He found acetaminophen with codeine and popped a couple of tablets. Pocketing the bottle, he went searching for more. He found injectables he was tempted to try, but remembering they were in the middle of a battle, decided not to do so. At least not yet. He slid a vial into his pocket just in case he needed it later. On the floor, he found one of those packs that turned cold when you smack it, and he whacked it on the counter and held it over his throbbing knuckles.

If there were a couch in here, he would have laid down for a minute. Given the meds time to kick in. He thought about lying down somewhere and resting his injured hand on his chest and laying the ice pack over the top of it. Maybe if he remained still, everything would stop hurting. A burst of anger shot through him. Real men didn't have to rest because they were in pain. Real men worked through it. Ignored it. He would not turn into a pussy that had to lie down when he got a splinter.

He went back out into the central part of the store and found soda on the shelf. He kind of wished it was cold. He took it into the meds room and opened the medical refrigerator. He could cool it for later. He laughed when the light came on in the fridge. There were already a dozen sodas chilling amid the bottles and boxes. He put the warm drink in and pulled a cold one out, holding it against his body with his arm so he could get it open with his uninjured hand.

The first swig tasted right just because it was cold, but after the second swallow he examined the bottle. Diet! Shit!

He tossed the bottle out the med room door. It hit the glass entrance door and sprayed everywhere. At least it was diet, so it wouldn't make things sticky like sugary drinks would. He watched with some regret as the remainder of the soda drained from the bottle.

He opened the fridge again and discovered that not all of the soda was diet. Thank God for that. He twisted off the top of a cola and took a swig. "That's what I'm talkin' 'bout," he said, and chugged half the bottle. He was feeling better now, his mood rebounding with the ingestion of painkillers and sugar.

He wandered into the store proper and began scanning the shelves again. He picked up a glow stick and examined it. There must be some use for it, but it wasn't what he was looking for. He tossed it back on the shelf and picked up a package of party favors. They were the things that kids blew into and a curl of paper unfurled to the sound of a horn.

He tossed those down too. Worthless. The old world was full of useless shit. He should toss it all in a pile and set fire to it. Not much worth anything now. Hair dye. Douche. He didn't have a clue what that was used for. A woman's thing was all he knew, what it was used for he didn't want to know.

There was a packet of combs in a clear plastic case. He had a couple of men who could use those. One box of an off-brand of toothpaste, and three boxes of Epsom salts. A thumb splint. The thumb splint made him think of his swollen hand, and he looked for something to splint his knuckles. There didn't appear to be a knuckle splint, or if there had been, it wasn't there anymore.

Did they make knuckle splints? He couldn't remember ever seeing one. He wondered if he'd broken anything else in his hand. Would the doctor have to set the bones? He welcomed the thought of that pain. Cleansing pain, although he knew he wouldn't like it when it happened, it would clear his mind. Bring him back to himself.

Where was Angelica? This was taking too much time. He picked up a greeting card that had fallen to the floor. "Thinking of you", it said. More trash. He thought about taking a match to the building. Fire was cleansing too. He looked around for a lighter or matches. Those were useful. Ergo, there weren't any left in this room.

It occurred to him that he shouldn't burn down this building because of the medicines housed in the other room. His hands itched, and he felt his anger building again. He had the need to ignite the building. Why not burn down the whole town?

He left the pharmacy. He needed to do something with all this destructive energy. What better way than to engage in the gun battle? He felt for his handgun and his hatchet. They both were there, ready to be of service. He smiled. He'd catch up with Angelica and join in the battle. He turned and strode down the street in the direction of the gunfire.

The door to Glen's closet slammed open, which took him by surprise. He jumped to his feet, the broomstick held like a sword, ready to do battle. What he saw surprised him. Even backlit, it was clearly a woman. She couldn't have been much taller than five-foot four, was dressed in tactical gear that didn't hide her curves and was carrying an AK-47.

She stepped backward out of the doorway and said, "Come on, Doc, time to go."

He followed her out, blinking in the afternoon light. He marveled that she could get to the door and open it without making a sound. He'd had no clue she'd entered the room, and he had been listening closely. He towered over her, but she was unmistakably the one in control. It was clear she was no stranger to the firearm she carried.

"What happened to the people upstairs?" he asked. "Did you kill them?"

"No, I didn't kill them." She laughed. "Why would I do that? They are under my protection. No, I only told them that if they weren't quieter, Terror was going to come up and shut them up himself. We could hear them from the outside."

He could see now that she was dark-skinned, Latina if he was to hazard a guess. Along with her beautiful milk chocolate complexion, she had large dark brown eyes and short black hair gelled into spikes. Glen wondered briefly where she got the gel. It couldn't be easy to find.

Glen felt the relief wash over him. The children were alive. So this was one of Terror's army of military enforcers. She was intimidating enough. He followed her out of the room and down into the foyer. There was a rack of rifles hanging on the wall there. She set her weapon on a dresser that was in the hall, picked up a gun, cracked it open and looked down the barrel. She pulled a box of shells from a drawer in the dresser and handed to him.

"Know how to use a rifle?" she asked.

"I'm competent," he answered. Even though he thought he was more than competent, a woman of her military experience might not agree.

"I'm Angelica Barrino," she said, "one of Tyrell Moore's generals. At least that is what he likes to call us. I'm glad you can use a rifle, doctor, because we are being overrun and we need all the shooters we can find."

"Who started this?" he asked.

"If you ask them, we did," she said. "These people used to be from this town, but they elected not to stay under Moore's rule."

Glen noticed again that she did not call him Terror, and wondered why. Perhaps she had known him before he was called Terror and couldn't make the switch.

"Every so often they try to retake the town. Some of their people get killed or wounded, some of our people get killed or wounded, we chase them back to their settlement, and they lay low for a while. Then there is something they need or want, and they come here to try getting it and taking the town back. It's boring. I'm glad we have you because our doc is drunk, and when the fighting stops there will be a boatload of wounded."

"Your doctor is drunk again?" Glen asked. "He was too drunk to practice medicine yesterday." At least he thought it was yesterday, being in the darkness skewed his sense of time.

"You misunderstand," Angelica said. "He's not just drunk now, he's always drunk. He's a drunk. Completely useless for anything but the most basic care. And even then, someone has to keep an eye on what he's doing. He almost killed a man giving him the wrong medication."

"I see," Glen said, and he did. "I've seen that before. The responsibility of having people's lives in your hands gets to be too much, and they turn to drink. Pretty soon they are always drunk."

"Did that happen to you?" she asked, looking at him piercingly.

"No, that did not happen to me," he said.

"So what did happen? By all rights, you should be holed up in a city hospital somewhere. They say the hospitals are the only place where there is any semblance of the rule of law. Because people need medical help, so they play by the rules," she said.

"I left medicine before the fall," he said, meaning the fall of civilization. "So, I wouldn't know."

"Why would you spend all those years training to be a physician and then give it up?" she asked.

"I lost my wife and son to a drunken driver," he said. "I

felt that couldn't recover from that, so I left. I already was living off the grid when the world ended."

"That explains it then," she said and changed the subject. "We are going out now. Try not to shoot our people. I know you don't know all of us by sight, so pay attention. Only shoot people who are shooting at you. We all know who you are. Any questions?"

"Can't the two factions sit down and talk it out?" Glen asked. "This bloodshed is so unnecessary."

"They are the ones who attacked us," she said. "Not the other way around. We are protecting our way of life. They could join us at any time, they just have to accept Moore's terms."

"What are those?" he asked.

"What he says, goes," she said. "That's it."

But Glen thought Angelica looked as if something wasn't sitting right with her. Her mouth was pinched, and she had her eyebrows drawn together. She wasn't altogether happy with Terror's rule of law. He wondered if it had anything to do with the woman, Anne, who'd been so severely beaten. Maybe that wasn't the only thing that was bugging her.

"Something bothering you?" he asked. "It's just that you had an odd look on your face."

"Not unless you mean the war that's going on outside these walls. The amount of time it's taking us to get back out there is bothering me. Are you ready to go?"

"It's raining. Do you have a jacket I can wear? I don't know what happened to mine," he said.

She nodded and left the room. Glen wondered why she wasn't soaking wet. She came back with a raincoat that was as big as a tent, but he wasn't going to complain. It would keep him dry.

"Another thing," she said, before opening the door, "if you get captured by the other side, I suggest you tell them you were our hostage and that we made you take up arms. They are not nice to our citizens. When they come back, if they come back, they often are missing parts of their anatomy. Understand?"

"Oh yes," he said. "I understand." And he did understand only too well what she meant.

CHAPTER FIVE

THE NEXT THING Glen knew she was yelling "Go! Go! Go!"
and he was running down the steps and out into the street.
Gunfire sounded from the end of the block as he ducked
behind a tree on the other side of the street. Bark sprayed
around him as a bullet hit the tree, but then Angelica
returned fire and was yelling at him to follow.

He ducked back out from behind the tree, running low,
keeping his head down. He wanted to be the smallest target
possible. He followed Angelica around the corner onto Main
Street and noticed the dead man on the pavement. She'd
killed him with a shot to the head. What must it be like to
have that kind of precision?

They ran up the street, keeping down, dodging behind
parked cars, telephone poles, and heavy concrete garbage
containers. Someone had filled one of the hanging baskets
with flowers, and as Glen ran beneath it, it exploded and
rained dirt and flowers on his head. He had a fleeting thought
of a young woman finding it after the battle and how disappointed she would be.

He followed Angelica as she sprinted across Main Street

and the grassy mall, to the open area in front of Town Hall. A group of the invaders was holed up, hiding behind the pillars that flanked the main entrance. He dove behind another of the concrete garbage containers, barely avoiding getting hit. The bullet hit the sidewalk, inches from his position, rebounding to the left and sending a chip of concrete past his ear.

He wasn't unnerved, exactly, but he wasn't feeling soldier-like either. The flying bullets made him flinch with fear. He wasn't sure what he was fighting for, other than to protect his own life, and that he could have been more successful by staying in the closet. He didn't want to kill anyone, but if he didn't return fire, he had the feeling he'd be found wanting by Angelica. What would they do with their new doctor if he didn't prove himself in battle? Keep him prisoner forever? Or worse?

Glen rested his head against the rough surface of the concrete and dreaded the consequences of this battle. Angelica was stationed behind a light pole to his left, able to see every move he made. Not that she was watching him. She had her rifle to her shoulder and her eye on one of the men hiding at the top of the Town Hall steps.

He risked a quick look, men and women at the top of the steps. He corrected himself mentally. And he noticed a couple of them moving down the handicap ramp to the right of the stairs.

"To your right," he shouted to Angelica, "on the ramp." He heard the spit of the bullet as it exited her rifle and the thud as it hit its mark. This woman was deadly and he didn't know whether to be grateful or appalled. She showed no hint of emotion, not remorse nor glee. How could she be so without emotion in this life or death situation?

Probably she would say it was necessary to stay detached during a gun battle. You didn't want your brain distracted by fear or the need for revenge. A clear head and a steady hand were your tools for staying alive. And everyone wanted to stay alive.

But not everyone could keep calm in perilous situations. Glen, himself, was having trouble focusing, a thing that was as second nature to him as breathing. Normally. But this was not normal. Not even close.

He felt exposed in his position. Anyone coming from the rear quickly could get a shot off and kill him from the safety of the grassy mall while he was watching Town Hall. He risked another look around. Not too far off, to his right and a little closer to the steps, was a dry fountain. There was an abstract sculpture in the middle, which probably used to shoot out water, that he could use as cover, and a three-foot wall around the outside that used to keep the water in the fountain, that he could hide behind.

Now he just had to get there.

He waited until Angelica fired on the building again and, hoping they were distracted, ran for the fountain. Bullets were flying. But he managed to leap the stone wall and take cover behind the statue without getting shot. He dropped to his belly and squirmed around to the other side of the fountain, where he lay in a partial sitting position with his back against the fountainhead, his head just high enough for him to peak over the wall and see what was going on. Water soaked through the seat of his pants, rainwater had collected in the fountain.

Concrete shards rained down on him as bullets found their mark in the statue above him. His forehead stung, and he reached up to discover he was bleeding. He wiped it with his sleeve so the blood wouldn't trickle into his eye. He could worry about disinfecting it if he made it through this alive.

He began wondering why Angelica had brought him into the fray. Wasn't he more useful as a doctor than a gunman?

Any child could be taught to use a gun, not that Glen was advocating for children to be put in harm's way, but a surgeon? He had skills that couldn't be replicated in the current situation. Perhaps they still were training doctors in the cities, but without pre-med programs and feeder universities, where would the candidates come from?

It occurred to him that he might be able to return to his work as a neurosurgeon if he traveled back to the city. They likely still were doing that kind of work in Philadelphia and, if not there, then in D.C. But did he really want to be back in the city, working under all that pressure? And it would be intensified in this reality. This cobbled together power grid could not be stable. What did you do if the power went out in the middle of a surgery that could only be performed with a camera feed?

He remembered his days in the operating room. His had been a teaching hospital, and observers would sit in a gallery that looked down on the procedure, and cameras took live feed that was projected onto screens mounted around the room. He was so focused on his work that he never noticed if someone in the gallery passed out or vomited in a bucket. Not everyone could watch the opening of a brain or a scalpel plunging in to remove a tumor or penetrate a cyst blocking the fourth ventricle. It was best for those people to find out early in their training that being a surgeon wasn't the best option for them.

Sometimes there would be applause from the gallery after a particularly tricky and successful procedure. And when you lost a patient, which did happen despite all the precautions, there would be respectful silence and bowed heads as they filed out of the room. He didn't mind the audience, but he preferred it when there was no one in the gallery. And better still when he had a skeleton crew. The fewer distractions, the better, and when he had "his" team, the doctors, and nurses that he'd trained and insisted on working with whenever possible, then he reached a Zen-like state. He could perform an entire surgery without speaking more than five works, three of which were "close, please, doctor."

Those days were long gone, and it had been many months since he'd even thought of them. But still, though he had stopped performing surgery, he had more value as a doctor, so why put him at risk? Was this a test? And if so, was it Angelica who was testing him, or Terror?

That's when he began to get angry. God bless it! Didn't they know what they'd be losing if he got killed out here? They'd made it clear that their other doctor was a drunk, yet he'd put money on where to find him, and it wouldn't be on the battlefield. Rage burned through him. He aimed the rifle over the retaining wall and fired, not caring if he hit anyone or not.

If he got out of this in one piece, he'd be telling Terror and his general in no uncertain terms what he thought of their stupidity. They were acting like idiots, for goodness sake, and neither of them struck Glen as stupid.

It was then he realized his own stupid mistake. He'd attracted the attention of the invaders with his rage-filled gunshots. A woman appeared on the outside of the fountain. He hadn't seen her coming because he was too low in the basin to see much, and he hadn't wanted to expose his head by taking frequent looks. All she had to do was to stay low, keeping the fountain between Angelica and herself. Then, as she got closer, drop to her hands and knees so he wouldn't be able to see her. She'd executed the move perfectly, and he'd fallen into the trap.

She raised her gun and took aim, but he had his rifle ready, and didn't hesitate. It was his life or hers, and he wanted to live. He aimed at her chest and pulled the trigger. She looked surprised for a moment as blood blossomed from her chest, her eyes locking onto his, then she fell.

The sound of clapping came from behind Glen, and he turned to see Terror standing in the shelter of the fountain, one hand wrapped and held tightly to his chest, while the other smacked against the bare skin of his arm, an injured man's show of appreciation.

A couple of things came to Glen at that moment. The reason the woman looked surprised was that she hadn't seen Glen in the shadow of the fountain, hadn't known he was there. She'd had eyes only for Terror. And Glen hadn't saved his own life, he'd saved Terror's. He hadn't shot in self-defense. Although at the time, he'd thought he had. He wasn't sure what he felt. He believed that when you engaged in a gun battle, you have to expect to die, even if you are a woman. Maybe especially if you are a woman. He wasn't sure.

But he couldn't quite grasp the fact that he'd killed a human being. It kept slipping sideways in his mind. For a moment he thought he should see if he could save her, but he glanced at Terror, who shook his head.

"She's gone," he said. Glen turned away and added vomit to the blood and water in the fountain's basin.

CHAPTER SIX

MIA LED Sally and Christian through the forest in the direction she hoped was the way she had seen at the top of the tree. Before she could get too worried about getting lost, they came to the road through the woods, and because the trees blocked the view from the town, they took the easy way. Mia enjoyed walking down the middle of the road as if she owned it.

When she could see the sky ahead, she led them back into the forest and aways away from the road. When she judged they'd gone far enough, she took them toward the town, arriving at just the spot she'd hoped for. They were hidden from the guards, at least for the time being, and they could move, bent over through the tall grass, and get to the town wall undetected.

There was a gate at the road, but they were headed to a breach in the wall. If she hadn't gone up the tree, she never would never noticed it, but she had, and it was their way in. It was an opening in the wall, but because the two ends over-lapped, it wasn't evident from the outside. The townies hadn't even posted a guard near it. She'd have to be on the lookout for other obstacles, though, because there must be something there. Otherwise, there would have been a guard. These people weren't stupid.

She motioned to the others to stoop low and led them out into the grassland that graced this end of the town. Maybe it was pasture for their animals, or perhaps they used it to grow wheat, Mia thought. Otherwise, it just seemed like a waste of land. If you aren't going to use it for grazing, you may as well plant some lovely veggies. Or an orchard, an orchard would be nice.

The grass tickled her face, and she had to hold her nose to stifle her sneezes. Maybe that's what it was for, to reveal burglars with allergies. She held an arm out to keep the grass out of her face and kept moving. They needed to get to the wall and get through it.

They slowed as they approached. She was sure there must be a booby trap or an alarm of some sort. She was looking carefully, so she didn't miss the big ditch that surrounded the wall and was covered with a mat of woven grasses to camouflage it. Clever. There were probably sharp sticks down there, ready to impale the unwary traveler.

Christian and Sally helped Mia pull the woven covering aside and looked down. No pointy sticks ready to impale them, but a pile of bear traps so big she didn't think they could step over them. The ditch must have been dug with a backhoe, because it was at least six feet wide and ten feet deep. This was going to take some effort to overcome.

"We could climb down there, trip the leg-traps and toss them out of the ditch," Sally said. "That shouldn't take too long."

"I don't like it," Christian said. "What if one of us slips and falls? You could lose an arm."

"I'm not too thrilled about climbing down there," Mia said. "I'm not sure I could get back up again. I think we need to go back to the tree line and find a tree that's fallen, bring it back here, and drop it over the gap."

"Where do you think they got all those traps?" Sally asked. "There must be hundreds, thousands, if this ditch goes all the way around the town."

"I don't know," Christian said. "There must have been a storehouse or a manufacturer nearby. Otherwise, how the hell did they do this?"

Mia looked down. There were more than she could count between them and the other side. She shivered, they looked so deadly.

"Let's do this," Christian said. "A tree big enough to span the gap would be too heavy for us to carry, but if we collect branches and drag them back here, we can pile them over the traps. It won't matter if the traps go off because it'll just be wood and not our limbs that get snapped. My only worry is that the noise will attract attention."

"What if we threw a bunch of tall grass over the pile first?" Mia said. "The grass could muffle the sound of the traps snapping."

"That might work," Christian said. "I'll go back and bring tree limbs, you two tear up the grass and throw it down there."

So, they went to work. Mia helped Sally pull armfuls of grass, bring up the roots and dirt balls as well. Mia thought the dirt was probably a better dampener than the grass itself and started kicking the edge of the ditch to knock it down. Kicking dirt was easier than pulling grass out of the ground anyway. Together they were able to get a pretty good cover on the near side of the pile, but it was harder to cover the far side. They just kept piling dirt and grass on the traps, hoping they were getting the far side too.

Mia accidentally kicked a rock onto the traps. It landed hard enough to trip a trap. The grass may have dampened the sound, but it still made Mia jump. She ducked down, pulling Sally with her. They held their breath and Mia mentally counted to thirty before she inhaled. Nothing yet. She listened for shouts from the wall or footsteps, but the only sounds were the 'pop' 'pop' of the gunfire at the other end of the town. Maybe the bear trap couldn't compete with that. And perhaps, because it was at the bottom of a ditch, the sound didn't travel.

Mia didn't know for sure why no one came running, but she was grateful that she hadn't alerted the townsfolk. She sighed and tugged another clump of grass, roots, and dirt from the ground under her knees and tossed it into the ditch. Still nothing.

Christian came up behind them, dragging large branches with the leaves still clinging to them.

"Don't worry," he said, "from where I was it just sounded like a branch falling. Another noise in nature. With all that gunfire I doubt it even registered." He dragged one of the longer branches toward the ditch. "Help me with this. I think it might be long enough to cross the gap."

They scanned the wall for movement before standing the branch on the end of the limb that used to be attached to a tree and then letting it fall across the ditch. It reached, but only with the topmost branches. They were twig-sized and probably would break the minute one of them stepped onto the limb.

"Let me try," Sally said. "I'm the lightest."

Mia huffed. As if.

"I'm not saying I'm much lighter than you," she explained to Mia, "but I'm suppler."

"I don't think anyone should try crossing until we've added more branches," Christian said. "Why risk falling into bear trap hell?"

"He's got a point," Mia said. "You wouldn't want to end up

down there." She pointed to the ditch. "Especially the far side, where we might not have put very much grass or dirt."

They dragged over another branch, but it wasn't as long as the first. The high boughs rested on top of the first one, but didn't reach the far side of the ditch.

"But look," Sally said. She put one foot on the first branch, and one on the second, right at the edge, so her weight was on the near edge of the ditch rather than on the branches resting on the far edge. "They make a pretty good bridge. If we could get some long ones, like the first."

They performed their crouching run back through the tall grass to the edge of the forest and scouted for more fallen branches. Mia found a yellow birch that seemed to have a fairly tenuous hold on the Earth. It already was leaning at a sharp angle, so Mia pressed her weight against it to see if it would come down. It moved a little, so she went to the other side and tried hanging from the trunk.

Again, no luck. Mia started kicking at the high side of the trunk, uncovering what she could of the root system. Then she tugged until the tree leaned far enough over that she could scramble up the trunk, where she found a perch high in the air and bounced. The tree had a pretty good springing motion, and she had fun for a few minutes bouncing up and down. It was almost like a teeter-totter, except your feet never touched the ground.

What's the saying? It's all fun and games until the tree falls over? Mia bounced her weight hard, and that's precisely what happened. One minute she was riding a bucking bronco and the next she was on the ground, trying to figure out what had happened. She'd been successful, that's what had happened, and she'd hit the ground hard. There was no slow motion, gentle glide to the ground. Nope, she'd come down hard.

She laid on the ground, feeling dazed. She didn't even

have the energy to call out for the others. She stared up at the sky, watching the leaves of the other trees shimmer in the breeze, and wondering if she'd broken anything. Finally, her lungs started to function, and she sat up. Nothing was broken, but she wouldn't be doing that again in a hurry.

She let out a low whistle to get Sally and Christian's attention and tried lifting the trunk. It was heavier than she anticipated, but she was able to tug it along toward their path through the grass. She'd never make it all the way there, but she could get it started.

Christian found her first. "Nice find," he said, grabbing the other side of the trunk. It went much faster with two of them, and they were almost at the path when they caught up with Sally tugging another large branch. She had sweat on her forehead and was breathing in gasps.

"Leave that one," Christian said. "Mia found this tree, and I think it's tall enough to span the ditch."

"Fine," Sally said. "I'm all worn out from jerking this one along anyway," she said, grabbing the trunk farther down.

It wasn't long before they had the yellow birch lying across the ditch. They stood it up and dropped it next to the two they'd already placed there.

"So, we didn't have to cover the leg traps after all," Mia said. "We just have to cross this tree without falling off."

"The trunk is too narrow," Christian said. "Crossing that would be like walking a tightrope. We need at least one more of these."

"You don't think the first one we put down will do?" Sally asked, pointing to the limb that barely spanned the gap.

"I think if you lose your balance and put your foot down too hard, both you and the branch are going to land in the leg traps," Christian said.

Mia had been willing to chance it, but Christian and Sally convinced her that it would be much safer to have two trunks of similar size side by side over the ditch. So, she followed the other two back through the tall grass, even though she chaffed at the amount of time they were wasting.

It took much longer to find an appropriate tree this time.

They searched along the edge of the woods, but those birch trees all were well-rooted. Sally stepped in a marshy patch of grass and sank to her knee into muddy water. She almost lost her boot when Mia and Christian pulled her out, and she had to pull a leech off her leg, but that led them to a stream where several suitable trees were growing from the bank.

Once found they made short work of bringing the tree down and no one had to bounce on the trunk and hit the ground hard or fall into the brook. Mia, for one, counted that as a win. They carried it back to the ditch, dropped it into place next to the other trunk and branches, and were over the ditch and away in just a few minutes.

As far as they knew, no one had spotted them.

It didn't take long to reach the fence, which at this location was a ten-foot-tall stretch of corrugated metal with the bottom edge sunk into the ground. They walked east along the wall until they found what Mia had seen from the top of the tree, an overlap in the fence with a gap big enough to squeeze through.

Squeeze through they did, being careful to peek around the edge that led into the town to make sure no one was watching. There was a stretch of grassy field and then back-yards filled with gardens, solar panels, and windmills. The backs of the houses, with their blackened windows, looked as if they were watching, but there were no faces visible, so the three ran for it.

They vaulted a backyard fence, a low three rail fence that was more of a visual delineation than deterrent to entry, and then ran between the two houses. They stopped before emerging out into the front yards and had a whispered argument about what to do next. Mia thought they should go straight to the library, as that was where she had seen Glen last, but Christian and Sally figured they should start right here and search, house by house, all the way across town.

"That will take us forever," Mia said. "And the longer we are here, the more likely we are to get caught."

Sally and Christian looked at each other.

"Mia has a point," Sally said. "How likely are we to find him in a random house?"

"Okay," Christian said. "Library first, and we'll see where that leads us."

"I just hope he's not where the worst of the fighting is," Mia said. "That could be a disaster."

"Do you think you can find the library?" Christian asked.

"It's not that big of a town," Mia said, "and also I saw it from the top of the tree. So, I have a good idea where it is. Luckily, most people are hiding from the gunfire. So, we should be undetected. Are you ready?"

Sally and Christian nodded their assent. Mia jogged out from between the houses, around the gardens in the front yard, and out into the street, where she headed to the right. At the first cross street, she took a left. Sally and Christian flanked her. They ran undetected for a couple of more blocks, and then Sally took them to the right again. A block down was the library.

They stood outside the big wooden double doors for what seemed to Mia like hours but was probably less than five minutes. No sound came from within. They pushed open the door on the left and let themselves in, carefully closing the door behind them. Mia led them through the cavernous entry hall to a room on the right that housed some of the books.

There were maps spread on a table, but no sign of Glen nor anyone else. They examined the plans on the table and

Mia had a brief and irrational thought that there might be a Post-It note with the words 'Glen is here," penned on it. No such luck, and the map didn't really seem to be of the town anyway.

They made their way back out into the entrance hall, where Sally spotted the blood on the column. They went to look and found blood on the floor as well. Someone must have stepped in it, because there was a trail leading out the back of the library. They followed it to the house next door.

There they found signs of a medical intervention, or at least a quick clean-up and bandaging. There was a damp rag that had been carefully placed on the edge of the kitchen sink to dry. In the trash were the kinds of detritus that comes from cleaning and bandaging a wound, bits of medical tape and the empty packaging from a roll of gauze, as well as a couple of leftover end pieces of the dressing itself.

"So, where to from here?" Christian asked. "Do we start our house to house search here?"

"No," Mia said thoughtfully. "I think it would be wise to search this house, but then I think we should go to the pharmacy."

"The pharmacy? Why go there?" Sally asked.

"Because I don't see any signs of antibiotic cream or painkillers," Mia said. "And I think with as much blood as was in the library, they probably would want those things. Maybe the general store is where they would go, but I would start at the pharmacy, because I saw both those things when I was there with Glen."

At first, Mia thought Christian was going to balk. His jaw tightened, and his face looked grim, but then he nodded.

"Okay," he said. "Let's get started with this house then."

They stuck together, which wasn't the most efficient way to search, but for Mia at least, felt safer. The first floor was most accessible because it was divided into four rooms, with no closets or places to hide. Kitchen, bathroom, dining room, and living room. There was a basement door, but they left that for last.

They climbed to the second floor, where they found a woman's bedroom, the closet full of military-style clothing, and uniforms. There were two dress uniforms with skirts instead of pants, but even without that, it was obviously a woman's room. There were high-heeled boots and shoes on a rack in the closet, hairclips, and scrunchies on the dresser, and decidedly feminine underwear in the top drawer of the chest.

Mia snuck a peek when Sally and Christian were examining the uniforms. They were figuring out the branch of the military they came from, and Mia was snooping in the drawers. Neither would help them find Glen, but it never hurt to have a look. There was a lovely gold and diamond necklace that Mia would have loved to own, but she left it. She had decided she only would steal what she needed to stay alive. Nothing more.

There was a bathroom behind the bedroom, and on the other side of the hall. It looked as though two bedrooms had been joined together to create one long room. It had been turned into what looked like a fitness room/dance studio. At one end was a weight lifting machine with a pile of different-sized weights piled on the floor next to it. On a low shelf, a bunch of free weights were arranged by size.

The rest of the room was empty except for the mirrors lining the interior wall and the dance bar that was fixed to the exterior wall. There were speakers mounted on the walls at the four corners of the room, and Mia wondered what sort of music typically came from them. But whatever device this woman used to store her music, it wasn't here.

At the back of the hall was a trap door with fold-down

stairs into the attic. Christian climbed up and poked his head through the opening. He came down frowning.

"Nothing up there," he said.

Mia led them down the stairs and back into the kitchen, where they found the door into the basement. "Maybe one of us should stay up top, so we don't get locked in," she said. "In case the woman who lives here comes back."

"I'll stay," Sally said. Mia let Christian lead the way down to a typical dirt-floored basement.

It was unlike anything she had ever seen, and so different from the basement apartment in her family's home. It was a plush in-law suite, where guests at their home had stayed in luxury. Here the furnace and the water heater were set on concrete blocks, but other than a jungle of spider webs there was little else. Mia was happy to get the heck away from the spiders. They left the house unlocked, which is how they found it. Mia would be surprised if anyone locked their home in a town like this. There was no point, really.

She led them out the back of the house and around the library, retracing her steps from when she'd escaped. They were moving toward the gunfire, which made her nervous. She'd never been fond of the noise firearms made. Where she'd grown up, a gunshot was not an everyday occurrence, and if you were in a place where you heard gunfire, you got the heck out. Here she was moving toward it. It was not a happy feeling.

And the streets reminded her of a ghost town she'd visited as a child. There still were bits and pieces of life scattered about, but no people or pets. She didn't see one face in a window, not one door opened to ask them what they were doing. She imagined the residents hiding in their panic rooms, or in bathrooms, huddled in their tubs, hoping they were safe from stray bullets.

She wondered how many houses held only children

huddled together while both parents fought to save the town. Society here might have reverted to a total patriarchy. That sometimes happened in apocalyptic circumstances. She had read about it in college. The primitive brain insisted on a more straightforward way of life that protected the children, and the women who could produce them.

Personally, she'd run far away from a town like that. She wasn't cut out to be property.

When they got to Main Street, they stuck close to the buildings, ducking into doorways when they saw movement. They moved more slowly now, carefully assessing each open space, every intersection. As much as they wanted to save Glen, they didn't want to risk their own lives doing it.

About a block from the pharmacy, they froze in place as the man Mia knew as Terror exited it. He looked both ways, but fortunately didn't scan the sidewalk. If he had, he couldn't have helped but see them. Terror turned away and strode toward the Town Hall, not bothering to duck from lamp post to lamp post to avoid bullets. It was as though he was daring the enemy to shoot him. But they didn't.

Mia noticed that his right hand was wrapped in a bandage, the blood beginning to seep through the white cloth. The fingers didn't look right to her, and she wondered if the bones had been crushed. Or maybe just broken? A shiver went down her spine, and she hoped her hand never looked like that. It must hurt like hell.

When he turned onto the street next to the grassy mall and disappeared from sight, she led Christian and Sally forward again. Having seen Terror made her think they were headed in the right direction. She would tell the other two what she thought as soon as they were safely inside the pharmacy. Unless someone still was in there. They'd have to do a survey before walking in blindly.

They made it in the pharmacy. Mia flattened herself

against the wall and looked through the glass door. Nobody was visible, so she pushed the door open, the bells above the door chimed, and the door rebounded. No one came out to see what was going on. No shots were fired. No one yelled. Mia shrugged and continued inside, followed by Christian and Sally.

It hadn't changed much since Mia had been here with Glen. The shelves were mostly empty and in disarray. There were more items littering the ground, but that was all. She turned to the others.

"I've only ever seen this floor, the store, and the pharmacy room behind it. I'm sure there is a basement and at least one floor above this. We need to search the entire building before we move on. How do you want to do this?" Sally looked from Christian to Sally. "Any suggestions?"

CHAPTER SEVEN

GLEN FOLLOWED Angelica and Terror back through town. The shooting had quieted down. There was only the occasional single shot or small volley of gunfire. The invaders must be either dead or retreating. Regular people were beginning to appear on the street, starting the cleanup effort for their town.

They passed the spot where the flower pot had exploded above Glen's head. There was a man outside the shop grousing about it. "Do you have any idea how much time and effort I put into keeping that flower pot beautiful? Adding aesthetic value to our town? One volley of gunfire and I'm back where I started. I don't even know if I can get seeds." He continued complaining as they passed, picking up what was left of the plants.

Glen held his firearm loosely, the barrel pointing at the ground, as they strode through town. Angelica still had her semi-automatic at the ready, but Terror appeared to be unarmed as well as injured. He cradled his gauze-wrapped arm against his body and avoided abrupt movements.

People called out to him as they walked by and he raised

his uninjured hand in salute, nodding as they passed. Those
same people looked at Glen with curiosity, wanting to know
who he was. He nodded at them as well but didn't bother to
raise his hand in a salute. They weren't looking for approval
from a stranger.

They passed the pharmacy on the far side of the street,
and he gave it a cursory glance. No one seemed to be
guarding it now. He thought for a minute he saw movement,
but it must have been his imagination because when he
stopped to take a good look, there was nothing. Most of the
other shops on Main Street had people in front of them
sweeping the sidewalks or washing the windows. Terror naturally ran a tight ship and cleanliness was required.

Terror and Angelica turned a corner in front of him, and
he hurried to catch up.

"You've got your town folk well trained," he said, gesturing
toward a family repairing a picket fence that had been strafed
by bullets. "They aren't wasting any time cleaning up the mess."

"That's not me." Terror said, shaking his head. "They are
proud of their town. Every time some group swoops in and
tries to take it from them, they fight back with everything
they've got, and then they clean up the place. It's like their
motto is 'Nobody fucks with our town.' They were like that
when I got here. It's nothing I've done."

Glen nodded but wondered if it was true. They may be
proud, but they didn't look particularly happy. In fact, the
family they just had passed looked grim. Then again, maybe it
was normal to be grim when you've been under attack. He
wondered how many had been wounded or killed, and who
was in charge of cleaning up that mess?

He followed Terror and Angelica to a home just on the
other side of the library, where they led him through the back
door into the kitchen. Angelica heated water for him while he

sorted through her first aid kit. There wasn't much there. He unwrapped the gauze from Terror's hand and frowned. He saw braded and broken knuckles and a nasty gash down the back of the man's hand.

He poured the hot water into a basin and added dish-washing soap. Then he had Terror lower his hand into the soapy water and leave it there. Terror grimaced and worked the muscles in his jaw. It probably was stinging, but too bad. The injury had to be cleaned, and this was by far the least painful method.

"Do you have any ice?" Glen asked, knowing it was improbable.

He was answered by Angelica shaking her head, "We have a lot of things, but ice isn't one of them."

"Do you know if you have any finger braces back at the pharmacy? Those would be handy." He pulled Terror's hand from the water and looked at it. The gash on the back of it was bleeding again. He splashed some warm water from the pan to rinse the soap away.

"Let me go back to the pharmacy," he said, gesturing to the hand.

"I need finger splints and butterfly bandages. Unless you think the doctor has sutures at his office?" He'd yet to see the doctor or his office. He somehow doubted the drunken doctor had a state of the art facility.

"Go with him," Terror motioned to Angelica. "And keep an eye open."

So, Glen and Angelica jogged back to the pharmacy, double-timing it. Glen kept his eyes open but didn't see anything new or helpful. Once in the pharmacy, it only took a minute for Glen to find what he needed. He was amazed that there were finger splints and butterfly bandages. The drunk doc must not have needed them.

"Do you have keys to the back room?" he said, motioning to the drug counter. "He'll probably need some painkillers."

"Truthfully, I don't think painkillers are a good idea for him." She pursed her lips. "He drinks a bit and has mood swings. I wouldn't want to add a narcotic to that."

"Mood swings, huh? Why am I not surprised?" He was going to continue with his concerns about Terror's personality issues, but Angelica's mouth had thinned into a straight line. Clearly, she did not want to discuss it with him.

"Oh well, then he'll have to make due with OTC meds like ibuprofen. They aren't as likely to cause problems with alcohol. Well, his stomach may not like it, but at least it won't cause mood swings." He thought a moment and amended his statement. "At least the painkiller won't cause mood swings. The alcohol is very likely to, but unless you want to start an intervention, I don't think there is much we can do about that."

She was looking away from him, out the window, so he couldn't see her face, but he took her silence for agreement.

They jogged back to the house by the library. Terror still was at the table, but now he had a glass of wine in his hand. That surprised Glen. He figured by now it would be all homemade hooch, or maybe some beer or ale if there were brewers in town. He was curious but didn't ask. The mood in the room had changed, and he didn't want to stir up things. Alcohol reduced people's inhibitions, and in some cases, personalities could do a complete backflip. With Terror, though, he was afraid it was something more, and he didn't want to provoke him.

He smeared antibiotic ointment on the wounds, closed the gash with butterfly bandages and wrapped the knuckles with fresh gauze. Then he splinted the fingers with the knuckle braces, taping the metal to his digits with medical tape. The muscle in Terror's jaw worked the entire time, and

Glen wondered if he should have insisted on something stronger for the pain. Well, it was too late now. He'd just have to hope Terror could tolerate discomfort.

Angelica tidied up the kitchen, washing the bowl and pan, drying them and putting them away. When she was done, they left the house and crossed over to the library. They entered through the back and Glen saw blood on one of the columns. So that was where Terror had injured himself. What had frustrated him so much that he'd felt the need to damage his hand on the marble?

Terror was somewhat of an enigma to Glen. On the one hand, he inspired loyalty among his troops. On the other, he seemed to have uncontrollable spells of rage. He'd appeared to be an understanding and compassionate man until he'd bashed Glen on the skull. He sought treatment for a brutalized woman but also was probably the perpetrator of the violence against her. Terror talked a good game, but obviously was emotionally unstable. The townspeople stayed, but they didn't look happy about it.

But this last point wasn't really fair. They had been under a great deal of stress today. It wasn't too surprising that they weren't dancing in the streets. You'd think that there would be a feeling of relief and maybe mild celebration after winning the battle, but perhaps too many people had died for them to feel anything but grief.

Terror led the way into the room where Glen first had seen him and took his place at the head of the table on the raised platform at the end of the room. Glen waited for Terror to ask him to sit before he chose a chair toward the middle of the table. Angelica sat on the opposite side of the table but up next to Terror.

A youngish man came into the room and hurried up to the table. He handed a paper to Angelica, nodded to Terror in a kind of salute and left at the same quick pace. Angelica read the note and nodded.

"Report," Terror said.

"Tyrell, we were lucky. Only three fatalities. Some twenty more wounded. Two of ours captured. We have four of theirs. All in all, not a bad exchange." She folded the paper and set it on the table in front of her, resting her hands on top of it.

Glen was surprised that Angelica had used Terror's given name, and he hadn't so much as flinched. She had some level of authority. He couldn't imagine any of the others he had met calling the man by anything but Terror.

"Do we know how many they lost?" Terror asked.

"Davis counted five carried away, but there could have been more he didn't see," she said.

"So we came out ahead," Terror said. "Good. Now we get to plan our retaliation."

"So, we attack them again? Tit for tat again? Come on, Tyrell. We can do better than this. Either ignore them or annihilate them." Angelica stood and paced the length of the table. "The status quo is ridiculous. They come here and kill a couple of us, we go there and kill a few of them. And then two or three of them will ask to join us, and a few of us will leave. Not all of our deserters go to them, but a number do. Meanwhile, we pick each other off. It doesn't make any sense."

"Are you saying my leadership doesn't make sense?" Terror growled. "Because if you are..." He left the sentence unfinished.

Angelica rolled her eyes. "Don't get your panties in a twist, Tyrell. No one is challenging your leadership. I'm just saying that, in my opinion, you spend too much time and manpower on those people. Bring them into the fold, create an alliance, or get rid of them. They are a distraction that you don't need."

Glen wondered if they even would notice if he left the room. He was superfluous to the conversation. Who possibly could be treating the injured? Hopefully, it wasn't the drunken doctor. He had no patience for this self-centered foolishness when there must be wounded to be treated. He stood up.

Both Terror and Angelica turned to look at him. The look on Terror's face was incredulous, Angelica sneered. He could feel them both willing him to sit back down. He did not.

"Where do you think you're going?" Terror asked.

"You must have wounded to be treated," Glen said, realizing as he did so that he'd made a mistake. He should have said "we." "We must have wounded," he amended himself.

"You'll not be treating the wounded, if there are any," Terror said. "I'm indebted to you, so I cannot kill you, but I don't think I'll be keeping you here."

Glen wondered what he had done to give Terror the impression that he was untrustworthy. He couldn't think of anything. Sure, Glen didn't accept Terror as psychologically stable, but he'd been doing a pretty good job of keeping that under his hat. Maybe he'd let something slip.

"Why is that?" he asked.

"It's clear to us that you were sent here as a spy," Angelica said. "The attack on our borders came too soon after your arrival to be a coincidence. Therefore, you must be one of them."

"But I just killed one of them," Glen said. "How could I do that if I was one of them?"

"What proof do we have that the woman is dead?" Terror asked. "It could have been a set-up to make us trust you more. We leave, and she gets up and takes off the body armor. She'll be sore for a few days, but nothing she can't handle. You could have staged the entire scene."

"I can't tell you how much I wish that were true. I'd be

much more comfortable with myself if I thought she was alive. It doesn't come easily for a doctor to kill." It hadn't seemed so at the time, he had acted on instinct. But now there was this horrible feeling in the pit of his stomach. He had broken the Hippocratic Oath. He had done harm. The one harm there was no coming back from.

But as he looked at Terror and Angelica conferring, he realized he'd better focus on keeping himself alive and worry about his immortal soul later. "Listen," he said, "I told you why I came here. Christian needed medicine. That was all. By this time, he's either dead or on his way to recovery, and hopefully far away from here. The others have no ties to me. Their plan had been to rob and kill me, before Christian was attacked by a bear that is. After that, staying alive was the priority. If you let me go, I will never darken your door again."

"Or," Angelica said, "we keep him captive and use him as our town doctor. One of these days our current doctor is going to drink himself to death." She stopped pacing and sat back down at the table. She tapped her knuckles on the wood. "Sit down," she said. "Let's talk."

Terror gave her a sharp look, but Glen sat. Staying alive, moment by moment, was the goal. Neither of these two seemed reliably stable, so placating them seemed the best plan of inaction for the moment. When talks broke down, he'd make a run for it.

CHAPTER EIGHT

SALLY HAD VANISHED back upstairs after the three of them had completed their search, so Mia went looking for her. She found Sally in a room on the second floor overlooking the street. She was standing in the gloom to the side of the window, frowning down at something. Mia approached, and Sally turned away from the window and met her halfway.

But Mia was curious, so she sidestepped Sally and crossed to look out the window herself. "What were you looking at," she asked. There were people on the street, sweeping up after the battle. One woman across the street was nailing a board over a broken window. Down the road, a small group of people turned the corner and disappeared out of sight. Was that Glen?

She turned to Sally and raised an eyebrow.

"Nothing," Sally said. "Just checking out the street to see if there's a way for us to get out of here before nightfall." She shrugged casually.

Mia thought she was just a little too casual. If that had been Glen headed back to toward the library, why wouldn't Sally want her to know that? Was she losing her nerve?

The women met up with Christian on the first floor. "I think we'd better stay here until nightfall," he said. "Now that the fighting has stopped, there are just too many people around."

They found a room at the back of the building that must once have been the staff room. There were a couple of over-stuffed chairs and a couch placed around a coffee table, and a TV in the corner. It was a reasonably comfortable room. The three of them set their weapons just inside the door and dropped into the vacant seats. Mia took off her boots and curled her feet up underneath her.

Mia woke to the sound of people coming into the pharmacy. She sat up quickly and put her hand gently over Sally's mouth. Sally woke instantly, her eyes wide open. Mia put her finger to her lips, went to Christian and woke him quietly as well. Then she went to the door and listened. It sounded like a cleaning crew of some kind. There was chatter and then someone trying to get the others to simmer down.

She slid out of the break room and took a peak in the back. There were people out there too, pulling weeds and sweeping the staff parking area. She slipped back in with the others. "Our best bet is the basement, I think," Mia said. "But we'd better hurry. And make sure you have everything."

She picked up her weapon and her boots and slipped back into the hall and across to the basement door. When they had checked the basement door earlier, she'd noticed it had creaked. She wondered if she should yank it open fast or crack it open slowly. When Sally and Christian were standing in the door of the break room, she cracked it open slowly, just far enough to squeeze through and slipped in. Sally followed, and then Christian.

Christian closed the door carefully, and they creeped down the stairs. They didn't dare turn on the lights, so they moved through the gloom. There were grimy windows at head height here and there, and Mia caught sight of legs and feet. She hoped no one thought to bend over and look in at them. There was a storage room in the far back, around the corner from a work area, and they headed for that.

There were no windows in the storage room, and Christian risked turning on his flashlight. He swept the beam around the room, stacked with shelves like a library, but full of cardboard boxes instead of books. Scattered among the cardboard were plastic storage bins. Mia wondered if she'd fit in one of the larger ones.

Christian walked the room, identifying three hiding spots. One under a table at the back, behind some boxes; one in a niche created by a shelving unit that didn't span the distance wall to wall; and one in an empty spot on the bottom shelf of a unit that was at the back, behind two other shelves. Sally slipped in under the table, Mia took the bottom shelf and assumed Christian had moved into the niche.

Then they waited.

They could hear footsteps overhead, and even the sound of people climbing the stairs to the second floor. Mia wondered why they had chosen today for pharmacy house cleaning. Maybe it was a post-gunfight ritual? She shrugged. Who knew why these crazy Stepford people did what they did? She didn't.

She was cramped, curled on her side, with no space to stretch her legs. She slid them out into the aisle between the shelves, figuring she could pull them back in if she heard someone open the door. It was dark and cold, but thankfully not damp. She wondered how long they would have to wait these people out. Maybe they wouldn't even come to the basement. But they did eventually. The sound of the basement door creaking open reached her ears, and then the footsteps down the stairs. There were at least four rooms in the basement, five, if you counted their storage room hiding place. Maybe they wouldn't clean every room.

Every contact point between her body and the board beneath her was aching by the time the door to their hiding place finally opened. Mia slid her legs back onto the shelf and curled into the smallest possible ball. A set of footsteps came maybe five paces into the room, paused and then went out again, the door closing. Was that it?

But then two sets of feet approached, and she held her breath again.

"This hasn't been touched since the last incursion," a woman said. "Which should mean that it's clean and we can leave it, what do you think?"

"I don't know. Half the reason we do this is to make sure no one is hiding in the town. This would be an excellent place to hide." This voice was male but seemed young.

"Let's ask the boss," the woman said. The door closed, and their footsteps receded and then climbed the stairs.

"Shit," Sally said from underneath the table. "We need to get out of here."

"Do you think they saw you, Christian?" Mia slid off her shelf, grateful to be able to stand and stretch.

"I don't know," Christian said. "Why don't you go over to the door and see what you can see. Take my flashlight."

Mia retrieved his flashlight with a minimum of bumping into things and went over by the door. "Oh," she said. "No, I can't see either of you, but we left footprints in the dust. So, they know someone came in and didn't go out again."

"Fuck!" Christian said, coming out of his hiding place. "We are well screwed. They'll be looking for us."

"Can we do something to muddle them?" Sally appeared from behind a shelf. "Like, erase the footprints, so they think they imagined them?"

"If there was only one of them, maybe. But there are two.

They'll back each other up," Christian said. "No, I think our best bet is just to get out of here and hole up until the search dies down. Then start looking for Glen again."

"I think he's back toward the library now," Mia said, looking at Sally meaningfully. "I think I spotted him from the upstairs window."

"And you are only telling us now?" Christian asked angrily.

"I wasn't sure," Mia said, "but the more I think about it, the more I'm convinced it was him."

"That doesn't solve our problem of where to go from here." Sally said. "And the longer we stand here, the more likely it becomes we'll be discovered."

Mia moved to the door, thinking if they cracked it open, they better could hear what was going on and make a plan. But the knob wouldn't turn. She tugged on it and tried turning it, but it was no good. They were screwed.

"It's locked," she said. "We're stuck in here."

"Who locks a storage room?" Sally asked. "That's insane."

"Maybe it originally was meant to be a cell of some kind," Christian said. "If the town didn't originally have a sheriff or police department, they could have designated this room for holding criminals."

"It doesn't matter, does it?" Mia said. "We are good and stuck either way."

"Not necessarily," Christian said, pulling a pocket knife from his jeans and stepping to the door. He opened the knife, but instead of a blade, there was an oddly shaped tool. He slid it into the space between the door and the jamb, wiggled it down, and two seconds later had the door open.

Mia turned back as she stepped through the door, "Should we do something about our footprints?" she asked.

"No time," Christian said. "And I'm not sure what it would accomplish. Come on."

He led them to the nearest basement window and peered

out. "No one out there," he said. "They all must be at the meeting to decide what to do about us."

The window was a narrow rectangle, high up on the wall, level with the ground outside. It didn't open, and Mia wondered if they were going to risk the noise of breaking the glass. But Christian pulled out his pocket knife again and opened the screwdriver tool. It took him less than five minutes to twist out the four screws and remove the window.

"You first," he said to Mia and created a stirrup with his hands. Mia stepped into it and found herself hoisted up and out. She wormed forward onto the gravel and grass, then turned to grab their gear as Christian handed it out to her.

Then came Sally. Mia grabbed her under her arms and dragged her forward until Sally's knees came through the window and she could crawl.

"How are you going to get out?" Mia whispered to Christian. "There's no one to give you a boost."

"I'll manage," he said.

And manage he did. He jumped up and grabbed something at ceiling height and then jackknifed his legs through the window. Mia grabbed his hands and helped pull his head and shoulders through.

"What did you grab onto?" she asked once he was safely through the window and they were picking up their things.

"A pipe of some sort," Christian said. "I'm lucky it held my weight. That could have been a disaster."

"There's no way to disguise how we got out, is there?" Sally asked. "Only they are going to know which way we're going."

"Can't worry about that now," Christian said, grabbing Mia's hand. "Let's go." They ran bent over, staying low, although Mia wasn't sure why. It wasn't as if they were running through tall grass or anything. Anyone looking was going to be able to see them regardless.

They ducked around a corner and then across the street directly behind Main Street. There was a tire shop on the corner, a large working area with a warehouse behind.

"There," Christian said, pointing. "We'll go there. I imagine there are a bunch of hiding places in there."

They ran for the warehouse, skidding over the gravel in the parking lot, but slowing as they reached the door. Christian went to open it. It was unlocked, so his tools stayed in his pocket. He cracked the door slowly, but hearing nothing from the interior of the metal building, he led the girls inside.

CHAPTER NINE

"I CAN'T KILL HIM," Terror said, "he saved my life not two hours ago. I can't break the code." He slammed his hand down on the table.

"Then accept him in or turf him out. We haven't got the manpower to keep a constant eye on him. And I'm not in favor of keeping him locked in my house." Angelica leaned across the table and grabbed his hand. She squeezed hard, and Terror looked at her in surprise.

"I need you to focus, Tyrell," she said, her fingers tightening until his knuckles ground together. "That man is hearing too much and seeing too much. If you think he's a spy from the camp, then you have to get rid of him. Send him back before he sees something that could really damage you."

"He's a surgeon. You do see what an advantage it would be to have a surgeon?" He looked at her, ignoring the pain in his hand and willing her to see things his way. After all, didn't it always go his way in the end?

"It's not an advantage to us if he learns something that gives them the edge and then he takes it to them," Angelica said.

"I am still sitting here," Glen said. "You could try talking to me instead of about me."

"You've cost me enough," Terror said, his anger rising.

"You had to come here and disrupt everything." He glared at Glen, willing the rage to subside. He knew that if he lost it here, he would lose all his credibility. This man had saved his life, and he owed him a debt of honor.

"You should leave now before I kill you." He stood up, enjoying the feeling of power he had towering over the man.

"You," he said to Angelica, "escort him to the wall. Make sure he walks away and doesn't come back." He glanced at Glen. "If he does come back, shoot him."

Angelica grabbed Glen by the arm, hauled him to his feet and dragged him from the room.

Terror dropped his head to the table. His head was pounding again.

CHAPTER TEN

ANGELICA LED Glen out of the library and out onto the sidewalk. "You know, if it were me, you'd be dead," she said. She walked quickly, and he had to quicken his pace to keep up.

"You've got to know I'm not with those other people. I never lived in this town." Glen drew his eyebrows together. He had lost his jacket, and it was starting to feel cold. He supposed he should be happy he still had his flannel shirt and his shoes.

"Doesn't matter," Angelica said. "You clearly aren't with us. You broke into our pharmacy, stole stuff. I would have killed you right then."

"And why aren't you killing me now?" he asked. "I can tell you want to." *Shut up*, he told himself. *Are you crazy? You're putting ideas into her head.*

"I do. I think letting you go is a major mistake." She shook her head. "But I'm loyal. And if you die on my watch, I'll lose his trust." She looked at him from the corner of her eye. "So you get to live, this time. But if I catch you out there in the woods, all bets are off."

Glen believed her and vowed to be far, far away before she

came looking for him. He hoped the three youngsters never ran into this woman. She'd eat them for lunch. Their chances of coming away intact from an encounter with her were slim. Her hand was curling and uncurling around the hilt of the knife she had in a sheath hanging from her belt. She wanted to use it, that was for sure.

They walked in silence along the road that led to Main Street. Glen wondered where Christian, Mia, and Sally were. Hopefully, far away from here. Maybe they had headed north like they'd had planned before they had met him. That would be good. Although the thought of never seeing them again gave him a strange feeling. He'd gotten used to them over the last few days. He felt responsible for them, which was crazy. They'd crashed on him.

He thought about Christian's wounds and wondered again if he'd asked one of the girls to slash him. Although, if that was the case, surely, she'd taken her job a little too seriously. Of course, he could have injured himself. It would be hard to control the amount of force you'd need to plunge a knife into your own gut. A shiver went down his spine. He didn't even like to think about it.

People were watching them walk down Main Street. They stood on their porches or in the doorways of the shops. Children watering their gardens stopped to stare, one boy so engrossed that he didn't notice he was watering the ground at his feet instead of the plants. Glen stretched his fingers into a wave without raising his hand, so Angelica wouldn't see, and the boy tentatively waved back. Children were the same the world over, he thought.

He saw a line of men and women with gunshot wounds waiting to be seen by the doctor. Or at least that's what he assumed they were doing. They looked pained, and many of them were holding bloodstained clothes to the bullet holes in their bodies. The more seriously injured likely already were being treated. He hoped the doctor wasn't drunk today, or more people would lose their lives due to incompetence.

He wondered if he should offer to help treat the wounded. It would be ages before the doctor got to these people waiting in the street. He turned to Angelica, "Let me treat them. These people are in pain and losing blood. I could cut down the amount of time they have to wait."

"Forget it." She eyed him curiously. "Always a doctor before anything else. Isn't that true? Unfortunately for you, I was told to get you out of this town, and that's what I plan to do. You can go treat your own people."

He wondered what she meant. Oh, yes. She was inferring he was connected to the other side. He didn't bother to correct her. There wasn't any point. Even if she believed him, she was going to keep up the fiction of his involvement with the settlement. It was such a waste of time and energy. He could be helping these people here.

They passed the pharmacy, where something seemed to be going on. There was a crew of people exiting with cleaning supplies, and a knot of men in earnest conversation standing in the street. One of them waved his hand toward the pharmacy, and his voice became a squeak. But Glen could not hear what he was saying. Something had them worked up. That was clear.

Then they were passing the grassy mall and the fountain where he'd killed the woman. That was going to haunt him for a while. Why had he thought she was aiming at him? It was so clear in hindsight that she'd been focused on a target much farther off the ground than himself. He looked away from Town Hall and hoped he never came to this town again. He did not want to be reminded that he had taken the life of a person who'd never meant him harm.

Finally, they came to the wall across the road that separated the town from the outer world. There was a gate here. Angelica unlocked it and held it open for him.

"I suggest you just keep moving," she said. "Like I said, if I catch you around here, your life is over." She looked at the sky.

"Night's coming. Better find yourself some cover if you don't want to be picked off. Our side, their side, common criminals. Plenty to be watching for." She closed the gate behind him. "Too bad you don't have anyone to keep watch while you sleep. The road's a dangerous place."

He started walking and didn't look back. No reason to tell Angelica that he wasn't planning on using the road. He'd stick to it until he reached the forest and then cut over to the path they'd come in on, head up to the top and back toward home. The road was not part of his plan at all.

He felt eyes on his back, a crawling sensation between his shoulder blades, and a voice in his head screaming at him to run. But he stayed steady. Walking with purpose, but not speed. You couldn't call what he was doing a saunter, but he wasn't running away. Nice and regular, and just keep breathing.

But the tingling sensation in the center of his back was hard to resist, and it was all he could do not to break into a run.

He breathed a sigh of relief when he reached the edge of the woods. Another 100 yards and he'd be out of sight, even if someone had followed him out of the gate. He didn't think they'd pursue him into the forest, where he potentially could ambush them. He thought they were smarter than that.

But he started to run just in case. He wanted to be far enough ahead when he left the road that they wouldn't know where he had gone. He jogged a few minutes and then risked a look back. There was no one behind him, so he jumped the shallow ditch and ran into the undergrowth beneath the trees, feeling the beginning of hope. He might just make it out of this after all.

It wasn't long before he began climbing the slope to the top of the bluff. He just kept going, as straight up the hill as possible. He was bound to run into the game trail, sooner or later, if he just kept moving. The higher he went, the more his spirits lightened. He almost couldn't believe he was going to survive this. And there was the game trail, another win. He stepped onto it and continued uphill.

Dusk was approaching when he started looking for the trail that would lead him southeast, toward home. He had hoped he'd get farther away from the town, but there was no point in traveling at night without a light. He could end up breaking a leg. There still was enough ambient light when he reached the fork in the trail to keep going. As long as he could make out the features of the path, he could keep moving,

But then suddenly there was something in his way. A dark silhouette that began as a mass, but then resolved itself into individuals. Several large men blocking his way. How could the town people get here before him?

He heard a sound and turned to see another group closing in from behind him. He thought briefly about running uphill through the trees, but he was almost guaranteed to end up injuring himself. The roots of trees, bushes, brambles, he wouldn't be able to see any of it in the undergrowth. So, he stood still, the hope draining from him, and waited to be captured and taken back to town to be executed.

A flashlight shone in his face and a voice he didn't recognize asked him who he was.

"Glen Carter," he said, and wondered if he should give more of an explanation.

"And what are you doing in these woods, Glen Carter?"

The voice was low and resonant, and Glen thought he might have liked this man, given other circumstances.

"I am heading back to my home south of here," he said.

"And where are you heading home from?" There was no impatience, just matter of fact information gathering.

"I was in the town." He was beginning to think he should just tell the whole story rather than make this man ask a million questions.

"Were you in the town voluntarily?"

"No, I was not. I was captured trying to steal medicine from the pharmacy. I think they wanted to keep me there because I am a trained doctor, but the leader didn't trust me. He would have killed me, but I saved his life, so he felt honor bound to let me go. However, one of his generals told me that if they caught me in the woods, they would kill me. So, if that's what you are here for, please get it over with. I'm tired."

There was a murmur from behind him, and a tall, broad-shouldered man stepped forward.

"We are not from the town," he said, "and I think you'd better come with us."

"You aren't taking him back to the settlement, Jonno?" It was a high, immature voice filled with anxiety.

"No, Beckett, I'm not going to take him home. But there are better places for questions than this. And we need Eric too." Jonno turned his attention back to Glen. "Will you come with us, or do we have to force you?"

"I'll come," Glen said, trying a smile, but even he could tell it was weak. "You can't be any worse than where I just was."

They let him walk unmolested, leading him back the way they had come, but just when Glen thought they were taking him back to town, they split off of the main path onto a much narrower trail that wound along the side of the hill. He figured they were traveling roughly parallel to the road that ran through the town, maybe two miles from it. A mile of forest and a mile of the hill. Maybe. It probably wasn't that even.

The one benefit was now that he was traveling in a group, he felt he was unlikely to be dragged back to the town and killed. And, as long as he cooperated, he was being treated like a human being. No ropes or gags. That was a plus. As they marched through the layers of leaves, he worried about his kids and where they might be. He hoped like hell they weren't in the town.

An hour later they came to a barn in a clearing. It was lit with lanterns, and a couple of rings of hay bales had provided a place to sit in the middle of the barn. It looked like a back-woods version of Town Hall. There was a fire pit in the center of the ring, but no fire had been lit that night. The fires prob-ably were reserved for celebrations, he thought.

Jonno waved a hand at the hay bales. "Take a seat," he said. "It may take a while for Eric to arrive. I sent someone off to fetch him, but it's a bit of a hike."

"Can you tell me why you attacked the town, while we're waiting? I'd like to know your story." He also was hoping for an explanation that would ease the guilt he felt over killing the woman. Not that he was hopeful that he'd get it. It would have to be one fantastic story to take away the remorse he felt over that.

"We needed supplies and food," Jonno said. "It was a raiding party."

"That was a lot of firepower for a raiding party," Glen said. "I thought it was some kind of vendetta."

"You'd be at least partly right in thinking so." Jonno sat on a bale adjacent to Glen's.

"We used to live in that town. Terror, he calls himself, he came roaring into town one day in a convoy of jeeps and pickups, kills a bunch of the men. Anyone who had the balls to go up against him gets shot. He runs all the lawmen out of town, sheriffs and town police both. Once we figured out who he was gunning for, we grabbed our families and took off. All the officers, firefighters, anyone with any authority. He offered to let the female officers and firefighters stay, but none of them would. They could see what kind of man he was.

"One of the guys had a farm outside of town, so that's where we settled. And we've done okay, for the most part. But we don't have a supply of medicine, and we run low on fresh food. They didn't offer us any of the power generating gear they had stolen. They kept it all for themselves, didn't they?" He rubbed an eyebrow. "Truthfully, we'd probably raid the town every so often, even if we didn't need anything. One of these days, we'll run those posers out."

"So, that's your town," Glen said softly. "They told me you'd left voluntarily."

"Yeah, he'd want you to believe that, wouldn't he? No, he ran us out of town, and he would have kept our families, but they saw what was what and snuck away that first day before there was any kind of real security system set up. My wife, Louise, she led the exodus. Spirited the children away in a garden cart covered in clippings. Told the soldiers that she needed to mulch some crops. My Weezy, she has such an innocent face, she took in all those tough men. I hear there were raging tempers when the big men found out. I'm damn proud of my Louise." Jonno grinned.

"How many families got free?" Glen asked.

Jonno shot him a look. "You are a curious man, Glen Carter. I hope you aren't planning to betray us."

"No, I really am just curious. You don't have to tell me anything. But having just barely gotten out of that town alive, I can sympathize with you. I'm only alive because of a fluke in his character. He can't act in a way he believes is dishonorable. At least until he's discovered that's the only way he'll get what he wants."

"Yes, I believe you speak the truth. Tyrell is an unstable man. And his generals are worse. That woman, Angelica, is ruthless and cruel. That she let you walk away is a miracle. I would have expected her to shoot my legs out from under me as I walked away." Jonno shook his head. "No, you are lucky to be alive."

"I can't disagree with that," Glen said. "Walking away from her I could feel her eyes on my back. I didn't dare to turn and look, but I was so thankful when I was finally out of sight."

———

CHRISTIAN OPENED the door into the big building, letting Sally slip through, then Mia followed. They waited as he came through and rolled the door closed. The interior looked like an old tire warehouse. In the shadowy light huge racks loomed above them, mostly empty, but here and there a set of tires still rested in their cradles. It was cold and dusty and didn't look like it had been used in a very long time.

"I can think of a hundred uses for a building like this." Christian crossed to a set of tires resting at eye level and ran a hand down one of them. "And yet they leave it completely unused. It's a waste."

Mia followed him down the center aisle. For some reason, Sally had gone to look behind a big panel van that probably had been used to haul tires. Mia guessed she was looking for likely hiding places, but she thought they probably should leave the town. They could stake it out from the woods, maybe get a glimpse of Glen and discover where they were holding him. She didn't like this town. It seemed like a trap to her.

Sally made a startled noise, and Mia turned back to see what was up. She found her around the front of the truck, gazing upward. Mia raised her eyes and gasped. There was half a village of people hanging from the girders. From the looks of it, whole families had been hauled up to die from hanging. There was a woman, Mia assumed the mother, surrounded by three children and a fourth in her arms. She somehow had reached the dying child and pulled it to her. But it had died anyway, there in her arms.

Mia turned away and bumped into Christian, who had been standing behind her. "It's awful," she said.

"Come away," Christian said. And then louder, "Come away, Sally, there is nothing you can do here."

Sally came, but she looked dazed. "Why would anyone do that?" she asked. "Kill entire families? Mothers and their children? My God."

"I think we should get out of this town," Mia said. "They'll kill us if we get caught."

"I agree," Christian said. "We should go back to the woods and watch for Glen from there. Or maybe we could get up high in a church steeple or something. We could see what was going on from up high."

"I don't care," Sally said. "But I need to get out of this building. I just want to throw up now."

"Come on, Sal," Mia said, leading her farther down the center aisle again. "We'll cut through and get out on the other side."

She secretly was hoping that once they were at the other end of the building, Sally would be able to tolerate staying hidden here until darkness fell. It was not smart to wander around the town during daylight. Especially since the gunfire seemed to have receded, and the townspeople could come out of their hiding places now. It would be so easy to get caught.

A noise like a hammer being dropped stopped them in

their tracks, and then Christian drew them over near the racks to stand in the shadows. But no one appeared, so they started forward again and finally reached a door. Christian cracked it open, but it didn't lead to the outside. Beyond it was an office space, and what might have been a sales display/waiting room. There were a few chairs scattered about, along with posters and odd tires that might have been on display.

There was a water cooler with a half-full bottle of water sitting in it. The water had gone cloudy, Mia thought, but then she saw that it was the dust coating the water bottle that was tinting it. Still, she wasn't interested in drinking it. She was happy to stick with the water in her canteen. No point in taking chances.

Sally picked up a magazine from the coffee table and flipped through it. She gave a cry of delight and sank down into one of the orange waiting room couches. "I haven't read this one," she said. "I used to love this magazine."

Christian and Mia looked at each other and shrugged. If an old magazine could keep her happy for a while, that was good news. The longer they waited to leave here, the safer they would be. At least theoretically. They sat together on another orange vinyl couch, and Mia rested her head on Christian's shoulder, wishing the world away.

How long could they survive in this world? Stealing their way from town to town? Could they go back to the house in the woods and stay there for a while? Would they be safe? She was just so tired, and she knew Christian need to rest so he could heal properly. And Sally? She was retreating into her head. Less and less communicative and never smiling. She remembered Sally as she had been in college, laughing and carefree. The memory caught in her throat and she was afraid she was going to cry.

A bang came from within the warehouse, and Mia sat up

straight. Sally was already on her feet, looking at the door back into the storage area with big eyes. Christian was up now too, moving to the exterior door. He stood to the side, looking out through the window.

The noise got louder and closer. Mia had the impression that people were banging metal spoons on baking pans, trying to spook them into running into the street. "Wait!" she said to Christian, but it was too late. He had unlocked the door. The door was pushed open from the outside, and a person filled the frame. A brute of a man, with a rifle in one hand and a military-style machine gun in the other. Bullet belts crossing his chest and a manic grin on his face.

———

PEOPLE HAD BEGUN FILTERING into the barn while Glen had been speaking to Jonno. A number of them sat on the hay bales and listened to them talk, while others stood at the edges of the barn, or leaning against stall doors, chatting in groups of twos and threes. Glen tried to count without being obvious, but he kept losing track. People moved, and others came to sit or stand in their places, but he thought there must be at least thirty people in the barn.

Beckett, the young man who'd questioned Jonno when they'd first met, came back with a tall, bearded, middle-aged man. He was graying at the temples, but he still was in excellent shape. Jonno stood and shook his hand.

"Glen," he said, "this is Eric Wheeler. He's our de facto leader. He was the sheriff in the town that was."

Glen stood up and shook Eric's Wheeler's hand. He had a good grip, firm but not crushing, and he looked directly into Glen's eyes. A straightforward man.

"Nice to meet you, Glen," Eric said. "I understand you

spent some time as an unwilling guest of the town? Do you mind if I ask a few questions?"

"Not at all," Glen said. "I understand the need to know who you are talking to."

"Sit back down," Eric said, and he followed his own advice, sitting on the end of the bale next to Glen's. Jonno flanked him, and Glen sat back down where he'd been.

"What can you tell me about the organization, hierarchy of power, if you will, in the town at this time?" Eric leaned forward, resting his elbows on his knees and listened carefully.

Glen explained about Terror, his three thugs, and Angelica. He wasn't sure if the thugs were 'generals' as such, but Angelica definitely was. He told the story of the attempted heist at the pharmacy and his reasoning behind sneaking in versus just asking for help.

"You were right, of course," Eric said. "He never would have given you supplies, and he may have shot you on the spot. But I'm interrupting. Go on."

Glen told the story of Mia's escape, his hope that Christian had found the medicine and lived, and his stay in the closet in what he assumed was Angelica's home. He talked of the people in line to be seen by the doctor, and his fear of being shot in the back as he walked away.

Eric nodded throughout and then sat quietly for a moment. He raised an eyebrow at Jonno, who nodded and then turned to look past Glen at a black woman who was sitting behind him. "They keep me honest," Eric said. "Monitor my instincts. They think you are honest, and I tend to concur. So, I'll tell you my story, and we'll see where we're at. Does that sound alright to you?"

"Sure." Glen gave one short nod. "I'm okay with that." His instinct was to like the man, and trust him. The fact that he relied on others to help him reassured Glen. There was something about Eric that reminded him of ordinary life. Steady and reliable.

"When Terror, I believe his real name is Tyrell Moore, came to town and started killing people, I smuggled out my family, and anyone else who wanted to come, to my grandparents' farm. This is one of their barns you're are sitting in. It's at the far edge of the property and makes a convenient meeting place. Anyway, I brought my family, my sisters and their families and a few others who could see the writing on the wall."

"Thank God you could see it," Jonno said, "or all of us would be dead."

"That may well be," Eric continued. "I got them here safe, and then I went back to see if this Tyrell could be reasoned with. I sat with him an entire evening and what I saw terrified me. There was no method to his madness, no reasoning behind who he killed and who he spared. At least none that I could see, and none he was willing to tell me. He offered me a place as one of his generals, but as he'd killed most of the first responders of every possible description, I didn't think the offer was genuine. But I asked him to let me think about it, and he agreed without reservation.

"We shook hands, and I headed in the direction of home, planning to head out to the farm as soon as I was sure no one was watching me. But it was clear within five minutes of leaving the library, that's where Tyrell had set up his war room, that someone was following me. So, I didn't go home, even though I would have loved to grab some of my gear. Instead, I dodged around a few buildings and hid in a shed.

"A few minutes later three armed men went by my hiding place. They didn't find me because they didn't know that I'd realized I was being followed. They moved on, and I slid out of town like a shadow. And two years later, here we are." Eric gestured to the people around him.

"But you attacked them today," Glen said, carefully not mentioning his part in the killing. "Why was that?"

"I think Jonno already told you that," Eric said. "There are certain things we need, and we go there to get them. It was our town, after all. And they are able to keep things fresh. We don't have electricity, and food spoils. What Jonno didn't tell you is that there are people still living in that town who'd rather have us back and Tyrell and his minions gone. They put food in caches in the forest for us. And they do what they can to fight on our side when we raid them. One of these days we'll figure out the best way to retake the town, without getting our townspeople killed."

"My God," Glen said. "I hate that Terror more with every word. If you want my help getting your town back, you've got it.

CHAPTER ELEVEN

MIA GLANCED around the room looking for a way out, but there were only two exit doors. One led through the warehouse, where there was a hoard gathering, and behind them, an area filled with families hanging from their necks. The other was an interior door, but she'd have to pass in front of the thug standing by the front door to get there. She wondered if it would be worth it to take the chance.

Christian moved slightly, blocking the line of sight between the thug and Mia. She took the chance, sliding behind a stack of tires and around a group of waiting room chairs before ducking through the doorway. It was a standard automotive office, an inexpensive metal desk, orange plastic chairs with papers scattered on a table in the corner. In the other corner was a ladder. Mia crossed the floor in three strides and scrambled up the ladder, pushed up the hatch and crawled into the space above the office.

She had thought it would be a low attic space, but of course, it was part of the larger building, so it really was quite tall. The office was a box topped by a platform that was used for tire storage. She stood and moved carefully to the edge, where she could peer around a stack of tires and see down into the warehouse. A dozen or so townspeople were converging on the office.

Then she took a few steps and looked over a row of tires balanced on their sides, a display for the shoppers waiting in the showroom. The thug had moved into the room and Mia finally could see him. He was big and hairy and dressed like a bandit from an old Western, bullet belts crossed over his chest. Christian was facing him, gesturing with his arms. Mia couldn't hear what he was saying.

Sally was cowering in the corner, hiding behind a stack of shelves. Mia tried to get her attention, but Sally was focused on the thug in the room. She left for a moment and went back to the warehouse, where the townspeople were beating and kicking the door to the office. Well, she could put an end to that.

She had planned to dump a single stack of tires on the people below, but the feeling she got when she shoved the first stack off the roof surprised the people below and was so satisfying she dumped all the tires she could reach. The cries of surprise and pain and the subsequent retreat down the aisles made her wish she could do it again. But she had to rescue her friends in the office.

Sally still was oblivious to Mia's efforts to draw her attention. So she snuck to the line of tires closest to the thug and pushed them with enough force that they flew through the air and struck the man. Sally and Christian ducked back behind a shelf at the far end of the office, where they were out of the way of the flying tires.

Mia would have tossed every last tire off the edge into the showroom, except the thug regained his composure and opened fire on her. She dropped to the floor, hoping the sheetrock and plywood would afford her some protection from the bullets. Scurrying away from the edge on her hands and knees, she noticed a hand grasp the side of the platform from the warehouse below. She maneuvered herself, staying low until she could kick the fingers with the heels of her boots. The result was a satisfying yowl, followed by a curse and a thud. The would-be hero had fallen to the floor. "Take that," she said and scanned the roofline for signs of any others foolishly trying to reach her.

Another hand came up, followed swiftly by a face, and she put a boot in his mouth. She was trapped. She knew she couldn't win, but she couldn't stop fighting, trying to get the three of them free. And maybe if she attracted enough attention the other two would get away. Two people vaulted onto the roof at once. Mia stood and ran through the tire racks to the far end of the platform.

She reached the far wall and scrambled up the metal ladder that made it possible to get to the uppermost tires. The warehouse was noisy now with gunfire and shouts, so she didn't bother creeping around. She swarmed up to onto the top-most row of tires. She flattened herself along two sets of truck tires, hoping they would conceal her from the search below.

A loud clunk reverberated through the air and the tires Mia was lying on began moving. She bit her tongue so she wouldn't screech, and looked around, trying to see what was happening. She realized the entire rack was built to rotate so that tires could be accessed from down below. It wasn't that her tires were going to roll out from underneath her, but that someone knew how the mechanism worked and was rotating the racks so they could find her.

As she came even with the roof of the office again, she rolled off the tires onto it and slithered away on her toes and elbows. She looked around for an escape route and realized she'd squirmed through the dirt and dust for nothing. She'd crawled right into the thug's trap, and he was looming above her, looking down. A scar above his left eye gave him the illusion of inquisitiveness, like he perpetually was asking a question.

"Well, shit," she said.

"Well, shit," he agreed, reaching down and hoisting her upright by the back of her shirt.

Her feet back underneath her, she yanked her clothes back where they belonged and glared at him. She was not going to show this yahoo fear, damn it all. She'd been through too much shit today. She put her fists on her hips and sneered at him.

"So, what are you going to do now?" she asked. "Handcuff me? Knock me over the head? Shoot me? What's it going to be?"

"Aren't you a little wildcat?" he said. His voice was deep and resonant, like you might expect a devil to have.

"I have no interest in carrying you out of here. So, no, I'm not going to hit you over the head, or shoot you. I don't have cuffs, so that's not an option. What I'm hoping is for you to walk over to the ladder, get yourself down it and join your friends out on the street. Do you think you can manage that without pelting anyone with tires? You flattened Dave, he hit his head on the cement floor and had to be carried to the infirmary."

Mia didn't trust herself to speak, so she nodded and marched in the direction the thug indicated. If she opened her mouth, she was bound to say something to provoke him, and as much as mocking him seemed the thing to do, she really didn't want to get the butt of a gun to the back of her head.

She climbed down the ladder and followed a relatively typical looking townsman out through the office, which now was littered with tires they had to pick their way around, and out into the street. She went to stand with Christian and

Sally, neither of whom looked any worse for wear. Something she couldn't say for herself. Her clothes were covered in dirt, and she was glad she didn't have a mirror. She was sure her face was a mess.

The thug barked an order, and the three were herded down the middle of the street toward the center of town. When they reached Main Street, they turned left, and Mia realized they were headed back to the library. She wondered why Terror hadn't taken over Town Hall instead of the library. That would be more official, wouldn't it? She supposed he had his reasons.

She took Christian's hand and linked arms with Sally. They may be down, but they still were alive. She had escaped Terror before, and she would do it again. She only hoped they could find Glen and take him with them. She realized she was exhausted. It had been a long day of walking, climbing trees, hiding, and running. What she'd really like now was a bath, some food, and a nap.

But those luxuries were probably hours, maybe days, away. They were prisoners, and the defiance that had filled her while standing on the office drained away. She kept up pretenses, not wanting the thug to see what a coward she really was. She kept her head high, her footsteps energetic, and her face in an attitude of anticipation, as if she was going to a Fourth of July parade and fireworks. She steadfastly refused to think of Terror.

The walk down Main Street seemed interminable, but eventually, they turned again and shortly after that they were coming up on the street with the library. She guided Sally and Christian up the walkway without being told. She'd been here before, and everyone knew it.

They marched into the marble hall and then through the door to the library. Mia immediately noticed that the exit through which she had escaped the last time she'd been in this room had been blocked by a table. Still, given enough time, that might be a viable avenue for escape. But if she was honest, she didn't think they'd be given the opportunity to escape. That ship had sailed.

Terror, who was standing in the raised portion of the room, turned as they entered. He watched as they were shepherded toward him and brought to a halt just short of the steps. Mia kept her face carefully neutral. She had the feeling things would not go well if Terror got the impression she was gloating over her previous escape. When his head turned in her direction, she cast her eyes downward, examining the floor in front of her. She must not antagonize this man.

"Mia," Terror said, "how interesting that you have come back. Did you miss me? And this must be Christian, the young man who was wounded by a bear, and your friend Sally. Too bad you didn't get here earlier, you could have said goodbye to your friend Glen."

"You let him go?" Sally blurted out, clapping a hand over her mouth. Mia thought that Sally had resolved not to speak to Terror at all. But Sally was closer to Glen than the others. She'd probably been unable to stop herself.

"No, girl, I did not let him go," Terror said. "He proved himself unwilling to become an asset to this community, so I had him executed."

Tears sprang from Sally's eyes and Mia bit back a retort. So they were too late after all. Had they come to their death as well? She bit her lower lip to keep from joining Sally in her grief. Damn it. If they'd only found Glen earlier, they could have saved him.

Mia noticed the thug looking her way and lifted her chin. She refused to let these people see her beaten. Remembering how her father had taught her to stand up to bullies, Mia straightened her back and strengthened her resolve. She stood a little taller and glared at the thug. The corner of his lip twitched, and Mia silently dared him to smile. Just try it, buddy, she thought. I will wipe that smile right off your face.

But Terror was talking again, and she turned her attention away from the thug and focused on his boss. Terror was ranting on about loyalty and obedience, and Mia noticed that his right hand was wrapped in gauze. He'd been injured, and she hoped it was his dominant hand. He'd be a lot less likely to shoot them if he couldn't pull the trigger. Then she realized that every person in the room had a firearm. All he'd have to do is give the command, and the three outsiders would be dead.

But it didn't seem like he was interested in killing them at the moment. His words were akin to a recruitment speech. Was he going to ask them to join his community? He was going on and on about how he had built up this town, when Mia knew for sure that he had invaded it. She supposed he meant the power grid and the gardens. And possibly the hundreds of bear traps tossed in that ditch. All that work for nothing. She sighed.

Terror pointed a finger at her. "Am I boring you?" he sneered. Sally gasped, and she felt Christian stiffen.

A jolt of fear went through her, but she held her composure. "No," she said, "it's just been a really long day, and I'm tired. Do you think we could sit down?" Out of the corner of her eye, she caught an emotion run across the thug's face. She thought it might be admiration. But surely not.

"You want to sit down?" Terror asked quietly, a deadly chill in his voice.

"It's just that if I don't sit down soon, I'm afraid I'll..." She let her eyes roll back in her head, her eyelids flutter shut, and she wilted to the floor. She regretted closing her eyes because she couldn't see their faces, but she'd just have to ask the others later. If there was a later.

A commotion followed, with Terror shouting orders, Sally

sobbing, and then sharp breath in her face and a hand smacking her cheeks. Farther from her someone was radioing for the doctor. Terror ordered someone to lock them in separate rooms, and Mia was lifted off the floor. She could feel the crossed ammunition belts on his chest and knew it was the thug. She hadn't seen anyone else using bullets as fashion accessories.

They stepped outside, and the cold air gave her goosebumps. "You've got balls, I'll say that for you." The thug's voice was barely audible. "But be careful, or you'll get yourself killed. The boss likes his women timid and obedient. I suggest you use your acting skills to keep yourself alive."

She kept her eyes closed and pretended she hadn't heard him. This man could not be sure she was faking it, and even if he was sure, that was no reason to give him confirmation. The question was why wasn't he telling Terror about her duplicitous actions? Could he be an ally? This was something she'd have to consider.

He was carrying her up steps, a screen door rattled, and then someone opened the inner door. Once inside they went immediately up a flight of stairs. The thug's footsteps were loud on the wooden steps. A door opened, and he placed her on the bed. She felt his breath on her face again.

"Remember," he said, "timid and obedient."

He left the room, the door closed, and she heard the lock click.

CHAPTER TWELVE

GLEN AWOKE to sunlight on his face. He was surprised to find himself in a comfortable bed with soft blankets and a pillow. This confused him, until he remembered he wasn't living in a closet anymore. After the meeting in the barn the previous evening Eric had led him to one of the farmhouses used by the outcasts and had given him a room to sleep in.

He'd had a bath with water heated in a wood-fired boiler. A young woman named Nellie had brought him clean clothes and had taken the dirty ones away. There even had been clean pajamas to wear after he'd been fed. It felt like pure luxury after the past few days.

There was a tap on the door, and Glen called out that he was awake and sat up in bed. Nellie came in bearing his things and set them on the end of the bed.

"Good morning." She couldn't have been more than sixteen or seventeen years old, wearing faded jeans and a faded T-shirt with a picture of a blonde singer on it.

"Breakfast is downstairs in the kitchen when you are ready, but don't take too long. The boys are due back from chores, and they eat everything in sight." She smiled at him and left the room.

Not wanting to miss breakfast, Glen jumped up and got dressed. His clothes were clean and faintly warm. He wondered how they had been dried.

Downstairs he followed his nose to the kitchen, where a large table was laden with steaming plates of food. Glen was dazzled by the array. Pancakes were flanked by sausages, oatmeal, scrambled eggs, and toast. Warm syrup and cold juice sat on the counter.

"Sit," Nellie said, coming in through a door from the outside. "Eat."

Glen obeyed. Piling his plate with foods he hadn't seen in years. Even before the power went out, he hadn't fed himself this well.

"Would you like coffee?" Nellie asked.

He nodded, expecting some approximation of coffee, such as he made at his cabin. But when it came it was the real deal. He looked at the girl in surprise, and she grinned at him.

"My uncle owned a coffee roasting business," she said. "When the crash came he borrowed a couple of panel vans, loaded up his product and all the unprocessed beans and brought them up here to my dad's place. I don't think we'll ever run out. And we use it to barter sometimes."

"I'd forgotten how it tasted," Glen said with a sigh of satisfaction.

The back door flew open, and a herd of young men came in. Glen guessed they ranged in age from twelve to twenty. He tried to count them, but they kept milling about, grabbing plates and food, and he couldn't keep track of who was who.

He was surprised by the number of children. Why had Terror sent them away? What harm could these children possibly do to them? Then he realized something else, Nellie was the only girl he had seen so far.

He waited for the majority of the boys to leave again, tramping back out to help with the things that kept the settlement running, before he turned to Nellie.

"Where are the girls, Nellie?" he asked.

She looked crestfallen, and her lips thinned into a tense line. "There are a few here, the ones we could smuggle out," she took a gulp of coffee, "but that bastard kept most of the girls, even the tiny ones. And, a lot of the women too. The men and boys were told to leave or be executed on the spot."

She plopped into the chair across from Glen. "I had my hair cut short that summer, and I was dirty from playing in the fields, so they didn't realize I was a girl. My dad grabbed me, and we ran. That was most of the men. Anyone who had children high tailed it out of there. Eric put me to work here in the big house. My mom escaped and now she runs the bunkhouse. We live with my dad, here in Eric's home."

"But there are some other girls? Where are they? What do they do all day?" he asked.

She looked at him suspiciously. "My dad trusts you aren't a spy, but you sure are asking questions like one," she said. "We keep them out of sight. They live in a different house, have a sheltered place to play and work in the women's house. I'm not sure it's a good thing to keep them all together. If that house ever is raided, we could lose them all at once."

"Well, let's hope they are well hidden, then," he said.

Why did Terror keep the women and girls? He had a good idea, having seen that poor girl Terror had beaten. He was sure, given her refusal to talk, that it had been Terror who had done it, and that she had clued Glen in. Terror had an appetite for violence against women that would require a steady supply of women to satiate. You could wear out a person quickly perpetrating that kind of abuse on them repeatedly. Terror would need a pool of women to choose from.

He found himself feeling vaguely ill and Nellie looked at him with concern.

"Are you alright?" she asked. "Didn't the coffee agree with you?

"The coffee is wonderful," he said. "It's the thought of all those children being pulled from their families that's made me feel ill. We need to take your town back."

"That we do," said a voice from the hall.

Glen turned to see Eric enter the room, followed by another, Jonno, whom Glen remembered from the night before. Nellie went over to give Jonno a quick hug before he shooed her out of the house. "Go check on the chickens, Nell," he said, and she did what he asked with a smile on her face.

"That's a brave young woman you have there," Glen said, watching Nellie leave.

"That she is," Jonno said and smiled sadly.

Eric and Jonno grabbed clean plates and sat at the table with Glen. There still was plenty of food. Although the pancakes were gone, oatmeal, eggs, and sausage graced the table. Eric salvaged a couple of pieces of toast from a pile that had been dumped off the plate onto the table. He sighed.

"I never seem to get breakfast before those hoodlums," Eric said. "One of these days I'll get a pancake. Just watch me."

"Nellie would save some aside for you," Jonno said. "All you have to do is ask."

"They need it more than I do," Eric said. "And I'm afraid that with my luck the day I asked for pancakes would be the day that I didn't make it to breakfast at all. Now that would be a shame, for any of Nellie's pancakes to be left uneaten."

"S'truth," Jonno agreed, shoveling eggs onto his toast. He folded the toast in half and took a large bite. A look of complete contentment crossed his face. "Lord, that girl can cook," he said.

The men ate quietly while Glen sipped his coffee, and when their plates were empty, Eric pushed his chair back, stretched his legs, and sighed.

"Now," he said, "what can you tell us that will help us get Terror out of our town?"

"First thing," Glen replied, "is that you won't win with brute force. They outgun you, they have more manpower, and they have physical fortifications. You are vulnerable during attack because you have to come across fields with little to no cover before you get to the town walls."

"That I already know. The only reason we come in guns blazing is to create a distraction. This allows a small team of people to infiltrate the town, gather information and supplies, and then get out again. I know it's dangerous. We almost always lose people. If they aren't killed, they are captured. But then we usually kill or capture one or two of them. So, it's even, more or less."

He took a sip of coffee. "Not that we can afford to lose people. But yesterday, for example, we were able to bring back two women and four girls. That's six people who are now safe from the violence that happens there. Six people reunited with their families."

"What did you get in supplies?" Glen asked. He was curious what could be worth the loss of lives.

"Food, mostly," Jonno said. "But we won't know for sure what else we got until the last patrol checks in. One group always waits twelve hours before making their way back. Just in case someone unwanted follows us back home."

Glen wondered what they would do with unwanted people, but he didn't ask. Some questions you just didn't need to know the answers to.

"Do you know how many people in the town are ones

Terror brought with him?" Glen asked. "I guess the better question is, 'How many of them are loyal to Terror and how many would switch allegiances if they thought it was to their advantage?'"

"In the beginning, he rolled through with about one hundred heavily armed mercenaries, but after he'd gotten rid of everyone who might challenge him, he sent most of those back to wherever he came from. My best guess is that he has a core of twenty-five of his most loyal people. Some have integrated into existing families and might fight on our side. But there are also many townsfolk who feel he's improved living conditions and they would fight on his side." Eric drummed his fingers on the table.

"And how many still living in the town are loyal to you?" Glen asked.

Eric looked at Jonno, who nodded.

"Between six and twelve," Jonno said. "But to be safe, I'd say six. There are a few I have doubts about."

"And how many here?" Glen asked, a picture of the settlement starting to gel in his mind.

"We have a hundred and fifty-six children, twenty-five who are old enough to fight, and thirty adults. We always leave ten behind to tend the children. That way there always will be a core of adults to carry on if we should be killed or captured."

"And always one of the leaders," Jonno said. "There are four or five of us who see to the running of the settlement. Last night we left Eric behind. Next time, it will be me, and on like that. So that those remaining won't be lost. The logistics of keeping everyone safe, and with food and water, aren't uncomplicated."

"I can see that," Glen said. "But now tell me. Why you are willing to give me all these answers? I could be a plant, for all you know."

"We are telling you because we know who you are. We've had scouts patrolling the area since the power went out. A lot of strange and horrible things are happening in the world, and we wanted to know who our neighbors were. We know about your cabin, and how you live your life. But even more telling, you performed surgery on one of our elders many, many years ago. That man vouched for you, as did his daughter." Eric took a photo from an envelope on the sideboard and slid it across the table to Glen.

He recognized the man instantly. "Harold Blackmore," Glen said with a slight smile.

"I liked him. Some people are dicks, but you save their lives anyway because even dicks deserve to live. But Harry, he was such a pleasure to work with. I was delighted with his recovery. His daughter sat with him every day, and every time she saw me, she thanked me again for saving her father. They vouched for me? Well, I guess I'd do the same for them." He pushed the picture back across the table with a sad smile. "I'm sorry they've ended up in such a volatile situation."

"See to it you don't make liars out of them," Eric said. "Why don't you come out and meet some of our people? See who you are fighting for."

Glen followed Eric and Jonno out the door into a farmyard. They picked their way around a flock of chickens and were followed by two baby goats. One of them kept butting his head against the back of Glen's knee, threatening to buckle it. But it made the children playing laugh, so he didn't chase the little creature away.

In the barn, Glen met two men and two women who were putting up hay. They didn't have bales, which is what Glen would have expected. Instead, two of them were using pitchforks to hoist the hay from a horse-drawn wagon into a large boxed-in area, like a basement room with no roof. Meanwhile, the other two were trampling down the feed to make more room. Eric introduced him.

"No bales?" Glen asked, puzzled.

"No fuel for farm equipment," one of the women said. "We have to do what we can with Jack and Betty here," She patted the horse closer to her on the flank. "We have what we need for cutting and raking, but not for baling. So, we gather it loose and pack it into the hay mow. It's how it was done before fuel-powered farm equipment."

Glen, Eric, and Jonno left the barn and passed by a garden where several boys were weeding. They waved as the men walked by and Glen couldn't help but notice they seemed content, chatting and joking as they went about their chores. They walked past hay fields and pastures, and then through the woods for about twenty minutes before arriving at what could only be described as a stockade.

Eric pulled a rope hanging from a hole high on the fence next to fifteen-foot-high gates. A bell clanged inside the compound, and a small window set into the entrance opened. A woman with bright blue eyes peered out of a wrinkled face.

"Oh, it's you!" she said cheerily and set about opening the gate.

The men slipped inside, and she closed the gate behind them, sliding a large branch into metal brackets to secure it. They were in a large compound, probably five acres in total, with a large farmhouse sitting on the back of the first acre. Glen could see a barn and several outbuildings located toward the rear of the fenced-in area, but the majority of the compound was hidden from view behind the house.

"You haven't visited in a while," the woman said, placing her hand on Eric's arm. "I hope everything is going well?"

"You know why we stay away, Mille," Eric said. "I'd hate to lead the wrong person to you."

"Yes, that might be disastrous for them." She laughed cheerily. "We're contemplating pouring hot tar on intruders."

"Millie, this is Glen Carter." Eric gestured toward Glen. "He's a talented surgeon. Is there anyone who needs seeing to?"

Millie shook her head. "Not at the moment. I thought for a moment that Father Clements might have appendicitis, but it seems to have resolved itself." She turned to Glen. "Not only do we house the majority of the girls here, but also the old and infirm. Anyone who might not be able to defend themselves."

"Wise," Glen said. "But what will happen if someone decides to swarm the compound from all sides? What will you do then?"

"We have plans," Millie said and stomped a foot on the ground. A hollow sound came from below, and Glen realized there must be tunnels or at least bolt holes below them. "I was a civil engineer," Millie continued, "I've put that training to good use here."

She led them into the house, where several women were sitting around a large dining room table across the hall from a living room inhabited by the elderly, injured, and pregnant.

"Where are the children?" Glen asked, wondering if Millie would be willing to tell him that detail.

But she smiled warmly. "They are outside. Some doing chores, others playing. The older girls watch the younger children in shifts. Everyone has a chore here. Even these lazy buggers help with food prep or mending." She gestured to the group in the living room, then led Glen and the others into the dining room.

CHAPTER THIRTEEN

THE WOMEN in the dining room all were introduced to Glen, although he was unable to recall the names when he thought about them later. He was welcomed and offered tea, which he accepted. They were planning for the winter, bent over a diagram of a barn.

"We are deciding which animals to house here with us," Millie said. "We have to consider not only our needs but the needs of the animals. We only have so much room for feed, and water freezes quickly. We are isolated out here during the winter, so it's a balancing act. We need to have enough to survive, but not so much that we can't take care of the responsibilities that come with livestock."

Glen drank his tea and listened to the men chime into the women's conversation. They paid attention to Eric and Jonno but didn't defer to them. And in the end, the decisions that were made were their own, although they did incorporate some of Jonno's ideas.

Glen thought that only made sense. Eric and Jonno didn't winter here, and these women did. They had the experience of living it, so they best knew how to prepare. There was some talk about how the raid on the town had gone, and then the men got ready to leave.

Millie led them out the back, so Glen could see the children. He was surprised at how many there were. It was like recess time at an elementary school. Or almost. You wouldn't find a five-year-old sitting in the chicken pen petting the chickens at a school. In fact, wherever he looked, children were playing with animals, petting and loving them. He supposed they were happy here.

They were led out of a smaller door on the side of the stockade and began their walk back. The men took a different route back, traveling past other farmhouses and barns, Eric introducing Glen to the people they met along the way. It seemed clear they had heard of him and there were no suspicious glances or unwelcoming words.

It was mid-afternoon when they made it back to the farmhouse, where the day had started. When they entered through the kitchen door, three men were sitting at the table, which was piled with bread, cheese, and dried fruit.

Glen thought he recognized at least one of the faces from his time in the town. He had been on the periphery of the group surrounding Terror. He was a rough-looking man, with dark hair and a scar above his left eye that made him look as though he had come across something he'd never seen before. The man was heavily muscled, but his expression suggested a sense of humor. Still, this man was no stranger to violence, and Glen was wary.

"Ah," Eric said, "my informants are back. Have you seen the last raiding party?"

"The raiding party hasn't returned yet," said a light-haired man with a crewcut. "And we can't stay here long. We thought you should know that Tyrell caught a group of three intruders, two women, and one man. In their early twenties, I'd say. And, if I heard right, they were looking for him." He nodded toward Glen. "He's got them in Angelica's house, next to the library. And he told them that you are dead."

A hot fury burned in Glen's chest. How dare he tell them he was dead. Then he realized that Angelica might have indicated to Terror that she'd killed him. She wasn't married to the truth. She would manipulate people around her as long as they let her.

The blonde man exchanged looks with the dark man, who Glen remembered. He dipped his chin in agreement, and the first man looked at Eric and Jonno.

"Tyrell is starting to come apart. He contradicts himself and displays big swings in mood and opinion. This might be the right time to move." He looked at Glen, "Especially if you want to keep those kids alive." He looked at the others. "Let's move."

They were gone quickly. Eric, Jonno, and Glen took their place at the table. "Help yourself," Eric said, sliding the plates of food toward Glen.

They spent a few minutes eating before Glen spoke. "Those three, the two women and the man," he said, "are my responsibility. I brought them here to find medical supplies we needed to treat Christian's wound. I made some bad decisions, and we ended up separated. I was hoping they would go back to my cabin, but obviously, they went looking for me. I need to get them free."

"That won't be easy," Jonno said, in between bites of food. "But if we take down Tyrell quickly, I think it's possible we might keep them alive."

"I notice you call him by his given name, instead of Terror, which is what he likes to be called," Glen said.

"Why give him more power than he deserves?" Eric asked. "He isn't Terror. He doesn't inspire terror. Loathing and fear perhaps, but not terror. We call him by his name. We don't humor him."

"Makes sense to me," Glen said. "I hope my friends didn't believe him when he said I was dead."

"How did you meet those three?" Jonno asked. "I thought you were a loner."

"I am, or maybe I should say I was," Eric agreed. "They turned up on my doorstep..." He told them the story of finding the three standing at his door, Christian bleeding from a gash in his abdomen. Of how they'd admitted to planning to murder and rob him, and how they had changed their minds when Glen had worked to save Christian's life.

"I'm glad he's still alive," Glen finished. "I wasn't sure Mia made it back to him in time. But if the three of them are together, he must still be alive."

"I'm surprised you still want to rescue them," Eric said, "after they admitted to their plans to kill you."

"They were stupid and scared," Glen said. "I don't think they really had the stomach for it. They may have thought they could go around killing people, but I doubt they could have managed the reality. Especially Sally. I think killing a human being would have broken her. She's the sensitive type."

He realized how stupid it sounded the minute the words were out of his mouth. Of course, anyone could kill if they needed to do so. Sally would have wanted to live as much as the others. It would have changed her, of course, but she would have done it.

"It's just something I need to do," Glen said. "I barely understand the impulse myself, but it must be done. I can't imagine going home and living with myself knowing I could have helped but did not."

"Fair enough," Eric said. "I won't turn down your help."

The three men jumped at a loud knock at the door. Jonno stepped over and opened it. Millie stood there with half a dozen women Glen had not met. They crowded into the kitchen and those who could sat on the remaining chairs. The others remained standing against the wall.

"We want to help," Millie said. "We are tired of being left behind with the young. We are capable, and there are more than enough of us to split up the duties. If you are planning a strike on the town, then let us join."

"Millie," Eric sighed, "we've been over and over this. If everyone who raids the town is killed or captured, there must be enough adults left here to run the farm. You know this."

"If it came to that, there are enough children..." she was interrupted by another knock on the door, this one quiet.

Jonno opened the door to a group of children on the doorstep. Glen noticed that they seem to range in age from about ten to thirteen. They also crowded into the kitchen. Now the room was uncomfortably full, with children sitting on the counters and spilling out into the hall.

"Yes, Jack?" Eric addressed the tallest child, a black-eyed boy with an untidy mop of dark hair.

"We don't want to be left out either." Jack spoke loudly, and his cheeks flushed. "We heard the moms talking about being allowed to help, and we want to help, too. We're big enough. We've all been hunting."

"Hunting an animal is very different than shooting a human being, Jack," Jonno said. "I wouldn't want to lay that responsibility on such young people."

Glen noticed Jonno was careful not to call them children. But Jack's face turned stony, and he refused to back down.

"We know something that could help," he said, a little less loudly this time, "and we won't tell unless you let us help. It's our town too," he added.

"What do you know?" Eric asked.

"A secret way into town," piped a smallish girl with a mop of light brown hair. "No one else knows."

The other children glared at her, and she clapped her hands over her mouth, her cheeks blushing.

"Come here, Ingrid," Millie said, and the child pushed through the bodies surrounding her. "If you have information that could help us, you have to share it. Even if we don't let you join the fight. You know that, don't you?"

Ingrid nodded her head, her hand still covering her mouth.

"No, Ingrid, don't tell!" Jack clenched his hands by his side. "We want to fight too!"

Ingrid removed her hand from her mouth. "I don't want to fight, Jack. I might get killed. Or a dead person might fall on me, and I'm so little I couldn't get out from under." Her eyes got big. "That would be awful," she whispered.

"No one expects you to fight, Ingrid," Millie said kindly. "But if you could tell us your secret way in?"

"It's little," Ingrid said in a small voice. "Only someone really tiny can get in that way."

"How tiny, Ingrid?" Jonno knelt beside the girl. "Could Jack fit?"

"Maybe." Ingrid wrinkled her nose. "I can fit, and Tim, and anybody littler than us."

Jonno stood up. "Thank you, Ingrid. You don't have to tell us. If we decide to let Jack and some of the bigger kids help, then you can tell us. But no one as small as you is going into town. It's going to be very dangerous."

"You should let me try," Jack said. "I might be able to get through. Then I could tell our people to be ready. We'd have the advantage on the inside."

"We'll talk about it, Jack," Eric said. "Take everyone back to the compound. I will come see you after the meeting and tell you what we have decided. Okay? I promise to let you know as soon as we make a decision."

Jack nodded, the air taken out of his sails. "Come on," he said to the other children. "We got to go back."

"But Jack," a boy at the back said, "you said we wouldn't take no for an answer."

"We're not," Jack said. "We're taking maybe. Now let's go."

"That boy is going to make quite the leader someday," Glen said quietly to Eric as the children filed out, downcast.

"If he lives that long," Eric said, but he was smiling. "He'll be a hell of a leader."

When the smalls, as Glen thought of the children, left, the grownups began again.

"How will you decide who goes and who stays?" Eric asked Millie.

"We've already talked it over." Millie placed a paper on the table and leaned in.

"Plenty of folks at the compound don't want to fight. They start the set that is left behind. Then we paired up skills. Joan and Betty both are willing to fight and both are good at bartering and figuring out what's surplus and what's not. So, we only take one of them. Don Hammond and Delphie both are strong enough to throw bales, so only one of them can fight. We've paired up everyone. Anybody with an essential skill who isn't duplicated must stay behind. We have a list of one third of the adults and older youths who will need to stay behind. Everyone else can fight." She slid the list over to Eric.

Eric took it and looked it over. "I need to think about this," he said. "Obviously, we could use the manpower, but I want to consider each person on this list before I give my permission. Can you live with that?"

Millie nodded. "I can, but I can't speak for anyone else."

"I have the right to fight if I want to," said a man standing against the far wall. "I don't think even you have the right to deny me, Eric."

"Now, Don," Eric said "I'm willing to talk to anyone in private who doesn't like my decisions. But before you run off and get yourself killed, can we at least have a conversation about what the settlement would be losing from my point of view? Would you be willing to hear me out?"

"I suppose," Don said, "but it's my life, and it's my decision."

"Fair enough," Eric said. "But it may not come to that. I just want to examine the list. Now, if you don't mind, I'd like you all to follow the children back to the compound. I'll be there shortly."

To Glen's surprise, the group filed out without complaint. In just a few minutes the packed kitchen went back to being empty, except for the three men.

"Now," Eric said, "we need a battle plan."

CHAPTER FOURTEEN

MIA HEARD the door close and opened her eyes. She was in a sparsely furnished room painted in a soft white color. A dresser and a chair sat across from the single bed where the thug had placed her. There were sounds of footsteps on the stairs, some going up, other going down. Mia thought it must be the thug who was headed down the stairs. And possibly two others leading Sally and Christian up the stairs.

She waited for the door to open, and the other two to be ushered in, but it didn't happen. She heard doors opening along the hall, then two doors closing. They were to be separated. Well, what did it matter? They were doomed anyway. Two sets of feet went down the stairs.

"Mia!" She heard Christian's whispered voice down the hall.

She ran to the door. "I'm here," she called back.

"Are you alright?" he asked.

"Of course. Haven't you ever seen me fake a faint before?" Mia stage-whispered through the crack between the door and the jamb. "I wanted us out of that room."

"Together would have been better." Sally joined the conversation from down the hall. "I don't have anything to pick the lock with."

"Don't forget they probably are listening," Christian said.

"I know," Mia said. "Do you think Glen's really dead? If they had his body, don't you think they would have shown it to us?" She turned her back to the door and slid down to rest against it. She figured she was going to be here for a while and she might as well be comfortable.

"Do you really think he could be alive?" Sally asked. "I'd hate to think he died trying to save Christian from dying." She let out a faint sob.

"You think it bothers you?" Christian said. "You should be in my skin. I feel awful. And for planning to kill him. I feel like such a chump."

"Well, I'm going to believe he's alive," Mia said. "Until proven otherwise."

"Me too," Sally said. "We still could find him. Maybe he's being held in the basement, and that's why we got bedrooms instead of a damp cellar? Do you think they'll feed us?"

Mia felt her own stomach complain of hunger. She sure hoped so. Starving to death wouldn't be her preferred way to go. She didn't like that they had separated them, and the fact that they'd put them close enough to talk was telling. She'd put money on there being a fourth room with someone listening in on them.

Not that they'd learn anything significant. But Mia could sew some dissent. The thought made her perversely happy. She just hoped the others would play along.

"Christian," she said, "where was it you heard that a convoy was planning on marching in and taking over this town? Was it north or south of here?"

"North," Christian said, automatically.

Good, Mia thought. He understood. Focus them away from the direction of Glen's cabin. Even if he was dead, his home was the most likely place for Christian, Sally, and Mia to go.

"And when were they going to attack? Because I think that's the best time for us to plan an escape." Mia had her fingers crossed that this would bring the desired results.

"Soon, I think," Christian said. "In the next couple of days."

"Shouldn't we warn them?" Sally chimed in. "We might be in danger ourselves."

"Nah," Christian said. "Let them figure it out for themselves. If they know it's coming, they might put us out on the front line to fight for our lives. Personally, I'd rather wait it out here than get shot up defending a place that doesn't claim me."

"Me too," Sally said.

Mia could tell she wasn't sure what was going on but wanted to help. Hopefully, Terror's people wouldn't be able to pick up on that. Or maybe that was okay. Just because Sally didn't know what Christian allegedly had heard, that didn't mean Mia hadn't. A little confusion couldn't hurt too much.

She got up off the floor and went to the window. Looking out, she saw she was in a room that looked out on the library. She could see through the windows on the second floor into what looked like a reading room. There was an old man in there, his head bent over a manuscript of some sort.

It was harder to see into the first floor. The book stacks terminated on either side of every window, blocking the view of the inner portions of the room where Terror held court. Maybe that was why he'd chosen that location. You'd have to go to a lot of trouble to find out what was going on inside. But that also meant they couldn't easily see what was going on outside.

That she could use to her advantage.

She undid the latch on the window and tried lifting the lower pane. It wouldn't budge. It probably had been painted shut. But no, there was something else going on here, a place on the frame that had been spackled. She scraped at the spot with her fingernail until the screw that was holding the window shut was revealed. It was the same on the other side.

She didn't have anything resembling a screwdriver in her pocket. So, if she was going out the window, she'd have to break the glass. She rifled through the dresser drawers, but found only clothes and a few pieces of cheap costume jewelry. The closet was the same. If there ever had been anything useful in this room, it long since had been removed.

There was a loose floorboard in the closet. Mia pried it upward, but before she could see if there was anything hidden there she heard footsteps on the stairs. She quickly closed the closet door and got back on the bed. There was a knock then the knob turned, and the thug walked in with a tray and a plastic grocery bag.

That there were still plastic grocery bags in use years after the last grocery had shut down was horrifying to Mia. Not surprising, really, but guilt-inducing. We'll all be dead and gone, she thought, and there'll still be plastic blowing around. She also was pretty sure the plastic bag did not bode well for her now.

"Lunch," the thug said as he put the tray down on the dresser. He looked her in the eyes as he put his hand into the plastic bag.

"This is not my idea," he said, pulling a bloodied button-down shirt from the bag. "This was Glen's," he said and held it up by the shoulders. There was a bullet hole in the chest and a large blood stain cascading from it.

Mia gagged and turned away from the thug. She could smell the blood across the room. So Glen had been killed. He was dead, and it was their fault. Her fault for not opposing that stupid plan. She bit her lip so he wouldn't hear her crying.

She heard the rustle of plastic, a few steps, and the door closing. When she turned around, the thug was gone. She let herself cry for Glen now. A flood of tears and a few sobs. How she hated this new world, with death everywhere and no creature comforts.

She sniffed, got off the bed and looked at what they had given her to eat. Piping hot stew and warm bread. It would be a few minutes before the stew was edible, so she pinched off a chunk of bread and popped it in her mouth. After listening carefully for an excruciatingly slow two minutes, she picked up her spoon and went back to the closet and popped up the loose board.

She looked at the cavity under the floorboards, but it was too dark to see anything. She wrapped her sleeve around her hand in case there were spiders and reached down. It was a shallow hole, which made sense because it was only the space between the floor and the ceiling below. Two things were hidden there, a Phillips head screwdriver and a book.

She knew immediately that the screwdriver was for the window. She wondered who had been trapped in this room and how they had managed to smuggle a tool up here. The book was a diary. A teen's, judging by the entries. She'd been locked in this room for transgressions against her parents, running away being the worst of these.

Mia flipped through the pages, looking for anything of interest and discovered a key tucked in a break in the binding. It was slipped into a pocket up against the spine of the book, behind where the pages were joined together. She turned the key over and over in her hand. It was old, the kind of key you found in old farmhouses that hadn't had their doors updated.

She pocketed the key and looked more carefully at the book. There wasn't anything else in the little pocket, and the entries didn't seem to have much variation. Mostly I'm grounded, poor me, and my parents suck. Well, she'd had two ways to escape, so Mia didn't waste much pity on the anonymous girl. And anyway, the girl wasn't locked in the room anymore, so she must have gotten free sooner or later.

Which was Mia's plan, too.

She sat on the bed to wait until nightfall. A woman brought her to the toilet in the middle of the afternoon. Then later she brought dinner. Mia wondered where her thug had gone. She felt almost bereft. Not that she liked him or anything, she was Christian's girl, but he'd displayed a sense of humor, and an appreciation for her. Mia felt that was a positive, even in a guy who sided with the enemy.

Finally, the house fell silent. There were no rectangles of light on the lawn below her window, and it seemed as though everyone either had left or gone to bed. She went to the door, slid the key out of her pocket and inserted it in the lock. She turned it, and the noise it made in the silent house seemed loud enough to alert whoever was standing guard in the house.

Mia had no doubt there was at least one person sleeping downstairs. She just hoped that no one was sleeping in the fourth room on this floor. She'd peeked in the open door as she was being led to the bathroom. It was a room much like her own. Sparsely furnished, with no personal belongings. But that didn't mean it was unused. She hadn't heard anyone come up the stairs and past her room, but still, she would be cautious. She slid off her boots.

She stood still for as long as she could tolerate, and then slid quietly out into the hall in her stocking feet, being careful to shut the door as gently as she could. Christian's door was on the other side of the hallway, a few feet down. She stood outside it, listening, before putting the key in and unlocking the door.

"It's me," she breathed before she opened the door, just in case he had been planning to attack the next person through the door. And sure enough, he was standing there with a post from his bed, which was one of the old-fashioned kind with fancy poles on the corners that reached three-quarters of the way to the ceiling.

Christian lowered the post when he saw her.

"Good thing you said something," he whispered. "I was going to impale you."

"I thought you might," she replied and gave him a hug. "Come on, let's go to Sally's room and make a plan."

They moved noiselessly down the hall and opened the door to Sally's room. She was on the bed and sat up sleepily as they entered. Mia gave her a disgusted look.

"What?" Sally asked. "I was getting my rest so I'd be ready when we broke out of here."

"Did you see the bloody shirt?" Mia asked the others. "Is it even possible that he still could be alive?"

"I don't think we should believe anything we're told here," Christian said, "but it doesn't look good. I think our best move is to get the hell out of town and never come back."

"Shouldn't we at least look to see if they've buried him somewhere?" Sally asked. "If they just dumped his body in a ditch, couldn't we take it away and give him a proper burial?"

"I think he'd want us to get away from this place," Mia said. "He came here to keep Christian from dying. He sacrificed his life. It will have been such a waste if we end up dead too. I think we need to get out of here if we can."

"My windows are screwed closed," Sally said, "Are yours?" Christina nodded.

"Yep," Mia said, "but I have this." She pulled the screwdriver from her pocket with a flourish. "So, if the windows prove to be the only way out, we can get them open."

"That's my girl," Christian said and wrapped his arms around her. "Where did you that from?"

"It was under the floorboards in my closet," she said. "So I swiped it."

"What were you doing?" Sally asked. "Trying to dig your way out?"

"No." Mia grinned. "I was checking out the closet and noticed a loose floorboard. After the thug left my lunch, I pried it up with my spoon and found this, and a diary. The key was in the diary, along with a lot of drivel about how hard life here was after being grounded by her parents.."

"Teenager?" Christian asked.

"I think so," Mia said.

"If I'd had a diary, I might have bitched and complained on the pages too. After all, we got ripped off. All those great technological advances are useless now. I was going to be a computer programmer." Sally said.

"Since when?" Mia asked. "I thought you were getting your degree in psych?"

"I changed a few times," Sally said. "Computer science was my last major."

"Can we please get back on track here?" Christian asked. "We need to plan."

"Why don't we just leave now?" Sally asked. "We could sneak out the front door while everyone is sleeping."

"I bet there is someone awake downstairs," Mia said. "I think maybe we should wait another day to get the lay of the land, and when our guards change. Stuff like that."

"You just want to see that hot military dude again," Sally said, snickering.

"Don't be ridiculous," Mia said, but her face flushed brightly.

"Shush," Christian said. "I think someone is coming."

The three froze as footsteps mounted the stairs. Mia realized she should have locked the other rooms behind her, but it was too late now.

CHAPTER FIFTEEN

GLEN WAS WORRIED. He found the battle plan complex, and he wasn't sure if that was a good thing or a bad thing. There were too many moving parts, and the timing had to be just right. He knew they wanted to avoid loss of life on either side, but there was so much that could go wrong.

Eric and Jonno liked it. They were enthusiastically hammering out details and deciding who would go and who would stay behind. Eric was convinced the plan would work, and Jonno agreed, so it was only Glen who voiced objections.

"It's too elaborate," he said. "Too many moving parts, it just increases the likelihood things will go wrong."

"I appreciate your opinion," Eric said, "but this is how we do things. Each part is independent. If one of the parts fails, the operation still will be successful. We just increase our odds of coming out ahead by adding independent campaigns to our battle plan."

"And what will you do if someone grabs the children who crawl through the pipes?" Glen asked, standing up and pacing the kitchen floor. "What if they hold them hostage? Quit fighting, or the children die? What will you do then?"

"Nothing," Eric replied. "What you are forgetting is that the children here are related to the adults there. They might say they'll kill a child, but when it comes down to it, an aunt or uncle will object. A grandparent will step in front of the threatened youngster. It's just never going to happen. If they kill a child from here, they'll lose the support of the people living there. And Tyrell knows that. He's not stupid. Any threat against a child is toothless."

"And yet adults die every time you raid the town," Glen said. The guilt from killing that woman weighed on him. Would he ever have the courage to tell these people what he had done? He doubted it. And the pain of that memory was crippling.

"Regrettable," Jonno said. "I lost my sister in the last raid. But she knew the risks and insisted on being there. I will miss her for the rest of my life, but we are fighting for the right to exist. The right for this settlement to rule itself and have access to the supplies we need. That is worth dying for. And who knows, my life could end tonight, and I'll be reunited with her."

Glen blanched. He hoped to hell that the woman he'd killed wasn't Jonno's sister. My God. He had enough guilt already without knowing and liking the woman's brother. He had to put that memory aside. They needed to regain the town for these people and regain those three foolish young adults. He knew it was unwise to feel responsible for the town or the youngsters, but he did, and there didn't seem to be anything he could do about it.

"We're going up to the compound to decide who to bring this evening," Eric said, rising from his chair. "You can come if you like, or stay here and rest up. It's likely to be a hard night."

"I'll stay," Glen said. "I've got some planning of my own to do."

"Fair enough," Eric said. "We'll meet here at dusk," and then he and Jonno slipped out the door.

Glen watched them stride purposefully through the yard and toward the path, then turned away. He thought he'd remembered seeing a pair of binoculars in one of the rooms upstairs. His were long gone, probably out in the woods somewhere, maybe still on the ridge where they'd watched the town. And he needed them.

He found what he was looking for and searched the house for someone to ask permission to borrow them. No one was around, and there didn't seem to be any point in asking the babysitters in the backyard. They were barely teens. So he wrote a note explaining what he had done and headed out the front door.

He followed the path they'd taken from the barn the previous night, assuming that would be the correct direction. They'd traveled in the dark, and he wasn't a hundred percent sure which way they'd gone, but he thought the settlement was to the south of the town. So he needed to head north, and that was the direction of the barn.

It took longer than he remembered to reach the barn, and once there he debated which path to take. Finally, he decided on the trail that ran roughly northeast. It looked less frequently traveled and that made sense to him. He was pretty sure the observation skills he'd developed as a surgeon were standing him in good stead and he was happy with his decision.

He started out energetically, with purpose in his step. The air was fresh and the forest beautiful. It felt good to have something positive to do. An hour later he began feeling some misgivings. He'd thought he'd at least recognize some landmarks by this time, but the trees were thick and obscured the view of where he was in the valley. Still, it was the right direction, he was sure of it.

Two hours into his walk he was wondering if he'd make it back in time for the rendezvous with the others. He'd be walking back in the dark at this rate. A horse would have been handy, or a mountain bike, but he trudged on. He had a purpose to fulfill. He stopped for a break and took a drink from a water bottle he'd borrowed along with the binoculars.

He looked at the ground around the tree curiously. He could see footprints, and scuff marks on a boulder nearby. He moved around and found a broken branch or two. Odd, he thought, but he could almost swear that someone had been up that tree recently. Not today maybe, but in the last day or two. He rested with his back to the trunk while he looked at the marks on the ground. He'd almost swear there were three sets of them. His charges? Could be.

The thought encouraged him, and he continued with renewed energy. He felt as though he must be close now. Fifteen minutes later he came out on the road and felt wholly vindicated. He was almost there now. He traveled the black-top, keeping his ears and eyes open for signs of townsfolk, until the undergrowth thinned and the landscape ahead looked as though it might be opening onto the fields that surrounded the town.

He slipped into the woods, following a path that ran parallel to the road, but just out of sight. It wasn't long before he was able to see the town through the trees. He turned left, away from the road, making his way along the edge of the woods, but far enough from the clearing so he wouldn't be seen.

He came across a stream where it looked as though a tree had been torn from the ground and carried away. Again, the three sets of footprints. He wondered what that crazy trio had been doing with trees, but he kept moving, leaping across the stream. He had his own mission to complete.

He had to admit to himself that he was enjoying this. He

felt like an operative, a spy for his country. He had to find out where they were keeping his troops, and he liked pulling one over on Terror. He wanted to get him back for how he'd smacked him over the head and kept him in a closet. That was just uncalled for.

The terrain began rising, and he climbed with it. Gaining a little altitude would serve his purpose well. Finally, when he felt like he had the right vantage point, he moved to the edge of the forest and found a portion of an old dry stone wall to hide behind. He knelt behind it, propped his elbows on the mossy top stones and peered through the binoculars.

He was looking at the north end of town. There were houses between him and his objective, but they had been built with large yards, and he could see the library and house beside it. That was where he thought the trio would be. Not in the house where he'd been held, because a family was living there. Besides, you couldn't really put three people in a closet. No, they'd be here, where there was space to hold them.

He'd been inside that house, and he had a feeling about it that he couldn't ignore. He trained his binoculars on the house and examined every window, looking for some sign that his people were there.

But there was nothing. The three must have known Glen would be looking for them. They were smart. They'd find a way to show him where they were, but there was nothing. He trained his binoculars on the library. Nothing there either. Nothing.

Was he wrong?

He watched the house until darkness began falling, dispirited by the lack of any sign of them. He had been sure they'd be there. He scanned the windows one last time and saw a light go on in the basement of the house. But that was all. The only sign of life he'd seen all afternoon. He felt stupid. He should have spent some time checking out other areas of the town. He should have been looking for signs that Terror knew of the coming attack. But he'd single-mindedly focused on what he'd believed to be a certainty and had wasted the opportunity to gain an advantage over Terror.

He could have kicked himself. He trudged back toward the settlement, wishing he'd arranged to meet the group closer to the town. He'd walk all the way back, turn around and do the trek again. He hadn't had his best day, that was for sure. He'd wasted precious time and added a ton of walking time. And now it would be in the dark.

He made his way back around the edge of the clearing, staying closer to the tree line this time. It would be too dark for anyone to see him under cover of the trees, and he could use every bit of light he could get to see where he was going.

He slipped when jumping the stream and almost landed in the water, but he was able to catch himself and ended up with only one wet boot to squelch along in. He tried staying positive. One damp foot was better than two, he told himself, but he could feel his mood souring. The futility of what he'd done was overcoming him.

When he reached the road, a shadowy figure was lurking on the far side. He stopped, trying to see if he recognized either someone from the town or a settler, but he couldn't tell. Should he move on, or should he wait? He could move back into the woods and cross the road farther down. He began walking away from the pavement when he heard humming and stopped.

He recognized the tune. After the talk in the barn the night before, when they were starting toward the farmhouse where he'd stayed the night, one of the men had been humming a tune. Now this man was humming that very same song. That couldn't be a coincidence, could it?

He stepped forward, trying to get a look at the man's face, and a twig cracked underfoot. He froze.

"Glen?" The voice was barely more than a whisper. "Eric sent me."

"I'm here," Glen whispered back, stepping onto the road now. "Who are you?"

The man met him in the middle of the road and held out his hand to shake. As he took the man's hand, Glen thought he'd either end up flat on the ground with a boot on his throat or he'd have a companion to travel back with.

"I'm Daniel, Jonno's older brother," the man said. "Jonno's older brother. Eric sent me to hang with you. He said there's no sense in you walking all the way back to the settlement just to turn around. Follow me, and I'll take you to our meeting place. I have some food there, and we can wait in safety and comfort."

"Great," Glen said, relieved, and he followed Daniel through the darkening woods.

He was glad for the companionship, all the more so because Daniel knew his way through the woods and did not hesitate once. If Glen had managed to make it back at all, it probably would have been after at least two wrong turns.

Daniel led Glen to a small cabin on the side of the hill that would overlook the town in daylight. They mounted the porch and Daniel took a key from his pocket and unlocked the door. They slid into an entryway between two doors, and Daniel closed the outer door before opening the inner.

Glen was surprised. They entered what could only be called a cozy living space. There was a fire in the fireplace and lanterns sitting on a coffee table and hanging above a small dining room table. The windows were covered with blackout material, which explained the absence of light from the outside. Daniel hung up his coat on a hook near the door and poked the up the fire.

Glen followed him in and sat on the rustic couch made of

wood covered in animal skins. Daniel sat across from Glen and sighed, stretching his legs toward the fire.

"This is my favorite place," Daniel said, "even before a battle, or maybe especially before one. I can relax here. Feel at peace."

"I can see why," Glen said. "The settlement seems like a pretty busy place, not much space for quiet and relaxation there. This would be a good place to gather your thoughts. It reminds me of my place. Smaller, but with the same ambiance."

"I'd like to see your place sometime," Daniel said. "When this is all over."

"You are welcome to come visit," Glen said, "if we all make it through this. If I don't, I hope that someone would take those three kids back there for me. They need some guidance. Someone to teach them the ropes of backwoods living."

"Tell you what," Daniel said. "If I survive and you don't, I'll take care of your strays, but if you survive and I don't, I'd appreciate it if you would keep an eye on my family. Maybe render medical help if needed?"

"It's a deal." Glen leaned forward and offered Daniel his hand. They shook on the deal that neither wanted to come to fruition.

CHAPTER SIXTEEN

IT WAS the thug who found Mia and Christian in Sally's room. He opened the door, which Mia hadn't thought to lock, and came inside, shutting the door behind him. "You are not really good at this kind of thing, are you?" He shook his head and took a seat on a hope chest against the wall across from the end of the bed.

"If you had locked the doors, I would have tried them, and then moved on," he said sadly. "But no. You left them unlocked, didn't even put pillows in the beds to make it look as though you were sleeping."

He stretched out his long legs in front of him. "You also could have put something in the window. So if someone came looking for you, they'd know where to find you. But you didn't. If I didn't know better, I'd say you scavenged for a living until you met up with your friend the doctor."

"We aren't scavengers," Christian said. "We're thieves. Bandits. We take what we need, and we kill anyone who gets in our way. We were going to kill the doctor when we were done with him."

"You run across the only doctor within miles, and you

plan to kill him because... why? You don't think you'll get sick or injured ever again? No one you know will need a doctor ever again? You need to think about resources. You need to take the long view. Now, an accountant you probably won't ever need. Or an actor, useless. Now, a surgeon, that's a commodity. He can barter for his services. You'd never be short of food. You've got to think." He shook his head, and his dark eyes pierced Mia, making her middle hurt. She was so foolish.

"So now I've found you conspiring to escape." He leaned back against the wall, dropped his chin and stared at them.

Mia felt herself starting to shake. Not from fear, she thought, at least she didn't feel like she was afraid, it was just the thought of the unknown. And maybe because it was clear that Mia had really, really screwed up. She was so clearly an amateur, and that was embarrassing. She bit her lip and watched the thug thinking.

"So, what should I do with you?" he finally said. "Any ideas?"

Mia stared at him in silence, her lips a thin line. Neither Christian nor Sally said anything, but she thought she heard Sally sniff. A glance in her direction revealed Sally's eyes were glistening with tears.

"It's not Sally's fault that we are in here," Mia said. "So, if you are going to punish us, then fine. Just leave her out of it."

She glared at him and thought she saw the ghost of a smile. She was having trouble taking his threats seriously, and that angered her. She should feel threatened by him. He was menacing and a part of the enemy camp. Hiding a smile was a trick. Trying to make her drop her guard. Or secretly laughing, that might even be worse. Thinking how little and silly she was. She realized she was making a low growling noise in her throat and made herself stop. No need to give him more reason to laugh.

"Easy," he said. "I don't have time to think up elaborate punishments for incalcitrant prisoners. But I will have to move you. I can't leave you here where you clearly are not secure. And that includes your blameless friend. You won't be nearly as comfortable, and there won't be any windows to leave signals in." He shrugged. "You'll know better next time. I'm telling you, I could give you lessons in how to be a hostage."

"There won't be a next time," Christian said, with anger and frustration in his voice. "This is the last time I'm going after a man just because he saved my life. It's every man or woman for him or herself. This is a bloody waste of time."

"Take it easy, Christian," Sally said quietly. "We're at a disadvantage here."

"Like hell we are." Christian pointed at the thug. "There are three of us, and only one of him. He's outnumbered."

The thug stood up and pulled a gun out of the top of his boot. He rolled his neck, which popped loudly, sending a crawling sensation down Mia's spine.

"Come on," he said. "Let's get moving before you all decide to jump me, and you end up hurt. On your feet, soldiers."

"I left my shoes in Christian's room," Mia said, lifting her pant leg to show him her stocking feet.

"It's on the way," the thug said, "but we'll leave them there. You," he pointed at Christian and Sally, "leave your shoes here."

"And what if I refuse?" Christian asked.

"Then I'll handcuff you. You'd be better off just leaving your shoes behind." The thug leaned against the door jamb. "Hurry up."

Christian glared at him but bent over to untie his boots. Sally's shoes were on the floor next to the bed. She got up and left them there. Mia took her hand while they waited for

Christian to pry the boots off his feet. She did her best not to wrinkle her nose when he did get them off as his feet stunk.

"Lesson Three of being a hostage," the thug said as he led them down the stairs, "Never take off your shoes. You never know when or where the chance to escape will come. If you have to put on your shoes first, you may lose the chance."

"Like I haven't already learned that," Mia muttered, and she heard him snort. What was it with this guy?

They proceeded down a flight of stairs, through the kitchen, and then down the second set of dark stairs into the basement. The thug flipped a light switch, illuminating a big empty space with a concrete floor and walls. Mismatched cells lined two walls, some which might have come out of a pirate ship's hold. They were thick and black, speckled with rust. Others looked new, like they'd been pulled out of the local sheriff's station. Some were small and apparently made for animals as a human couldn't stand up in them.

The thug opened the nearest cell and motioned Christian in, locking it behind him. Sally was next, but when he indicated to Mia that she should enter a cell across the room from the other two, she balked.

"What if I need to use the bathroom?" she asked.

"Should have thought of that before you went on a walkabout," he said. "Which reminds me, hold still. You, I'm going to search."

Mia seethed with rage as he patted her down, taking both the key and the screwdriver. He held the screwdriver at eye level and examined it. "This is a first," he said. "I've lightened many a captive of various weapons, but never before a Phillips head screwdriver. Dare I ask why?" He raised his eyebrow at Mia.

"The windows upstairs are screwed shut," she said. "It's too noisy to break the glass."

He looked as though he had a question or two more, but he didn't ask, just waved her into the cell.

"There's a hole in the corner you can use if you can't hold your piss," he said. "But it'll start to stink down here if you use it too often." Double-checking to make sure all the doors were secure, he flipped off the light and headed back up the stairs.

"Don't feel too sorry for yourselves," he said from the door into the kitchen. "You're probably safer down here than you would have been upstairs anyway." He paused and then added, "even without shoes." He laughed and closed the door, leaving them alone in the pitch dark of the basement.

Mia slumped down on the hard concrete floor with her back against the cell bars. She wasn't particularly eager to explore the space in the dark. Spiders were a certainty, and probably rodents, too.

"I liked it upstairs," Sally's voice echoed in the dark. "Sorry to be a complainer, but couldn't have we left well enough alone, at least until tomorrow?"

"It's my fault, Sal," Mia said. "I apologize for getting you yanked out of your warm bed to sit in the dark on a hard, cold floor. We'll probably all get hemorrhoids."

"Not me," Christian said. "I'm sitting on my jacket."

"My jacket is upstairs with my shoes," Sally said, "but I can sit on my sweater."

Mia pulled off her sweatshirt, folded it and sat on it. She didn't know why, but she had more than one memory of her mother telling her she'd get piles from sitting on the front steps when it was cold outside. She'd probably go to her grave not knowing if that was true. And if it was, how did her mother know? She banged the back of her head gently on the bars. Mia hadn't appreciated her mother when she was alive. Stupid.

"Do you think you could squeeze through the space

between the top of the bars and the ceiling?" Christian asked. "I noticed there was significant space up there."

"Not me," Mia said.

"I might," Sally said, "but what good would it do us?

It's a residential basement," Christian said. "There is bound to be some kind of an exit. Even if it's just a bulkhead, we might be able to escape."

"But how would we get you and Mia out?" Sally asked. "I'm not going out there on my own."

"If we could get Mia out, she might be able to pick the lock and get me out. But even if we could only spring you, you could go for help, Sally. You could do that."

Sally was silent, and Mia found herself wishing she was in the cell next to Christian's so they could hold hands. That would be a small bit of comfort in this dungeon. Sally and Christian could sit together for warmth if they needed to do so. There'd be bars between them, but they still could gain some warmth and comfort. Mia felt a stab of jealousy and fought to control it.

She could hear movement across the room, and at first, thought Sally was moving to be closer to Christian, but then she realized the girl was climbing. The rustling was coming from toward the ceiling.

"I might be able to get out," Sally said, "but I'm not doing it until we have a plan. It would be stupid for me to get stuck sitting outside of my cell in the dark. Imagine how foolish I'd feel when that jerk found me there."

"Yeah, alright," Christian said. "Got a plan, Mia?"

"It's kind of hard to come up with a plan when I can't see what the options might be," she said. "First, I think we all should examine the outer wall of our cells. See if you can feel a boarded-up window or a light switch, anything that might help us see."

She stood up and, using her hand on the bars to help her,

walked until she found the back wall, but not before she stepped in the hole in the floor and nearly twisted her ankle.

"Watch out for your potty hole," she said. "I stepped in mine and nearly lost my foot."

There were grunts of assent from the other side of the room. Mia ignored them and placed the palms of both hands on the concrete wall, feeling as high up as she could reach. There weren't any indications of a hidden window, no light switch, no electrical sockets. It was probably just as well there weren't any sockets, because with her luck today she would have electrocuted herself.

"I've got nothing," she said. "How about you guys? Any luck?"

"Nope," Christian said. He sounded discouraged.

"I might have something," Sally said, "there's a recess about the size of a basement window, but it's solid. Like a window was cemented over or something."

"Knock on it," Christian said. "See what it's made of."

"Concrete, I think," Sally said. "It's definitely not wood."

"So, that's a bust," Christian said. "Any other brilliant ideas, Mia?"

"Listen, if there had been a window, that would have been a brilliant idea. You don't like my ideas? Then come up with a few of your own." Mia sat down in a huff. She was cold and scared, and they were lucky she could think of anything at all.

"So, really, no other ideas?" Christian was coaxing now.

"The only idea I have will make Sally very unhappy, and she'll probably refuse to do it," Mia said. "So, there is no point in going into it."

"I might do it," Sally said.

"You would have to crawl over the bars," Mia said, "and you already said you didn't want to do that."

"What would I do once I was out?" She was interested now, Mia could tell.

"You'd search the basement for a window or a way out. You could creep to the top of the stairs and see if you could crack the door – or better still turn on the light. The switch is at the bottom of the stairs. Then we could see what the options are."

"Why can't you crawl over the top of your cell?" Sally asked. "You're braver than I am."

"My bars go all the way to the ceiling," Mia said. "I think that's why he put me over here. There's no gap between the ceiling and the cell. You're brave enough for this, Sal. Just turn on the light, look around a little, and then crawl back into your cell. If they come down here, they'll just think he forgot to turn off the light."

"Oh man," Sally said, sounding miserable. "I really hate this new normal baloney. I'd give anything to be back in college."

"You would have graduated by now, Sal," Christian said. "Just climb the bars."

Mia could follow Sally's progress by the sounds she was making. First, there was rustling as she climbed, then grunting as she squeezed between the bars and the ceiling, then a thud as she landed on the other side. A minute later the room was flooded with light and Sally was standing at the foot of the stairs, her hand on the light switch.

Mia looked around her cell, noting the lack of anything helpful, unless you considered a hole in the floor a useful item. It wasn't even big enough to pee in, there'd be urine all over the cell floor if she tried it. Forget anything else. She played with the lock on her cell door. She might be able to pick it if she had a tool. She'd have to ask Sally to search the nooks and crannies of the basement. Maybe there'd be something she could use. Better still, they might keep a key down here.

She craned her neck, trying to see beyond the stairs. This

end of the basement was swept bare, and there wasn't a bulk-head to exit by, but you never know what might be in the dark at the other end. Tools, an exit, food and water. Her stomach grumbled at the thought of food, and she wondered if Sally could creep into the kitchen and get them something to eat when the sound of footsteps echoed overhead.

"Sally! Get back in your cell," she stage-whispered, frantic that her friend should not be caught. "Run."

CHAPTER SEVENTEEN

IT WAS midnight when the inner door opened to admit Eric and Jonno, who brought with them the bite of approaching winter. They stomped their feet, blew on their hands, and moved to the fire to warm themselves.

"Too bad there isn't room in here for the rest of the crew," Jonno said. "Everyone has numb fingers."

"You should at least send the kids in for a while. They must really be feeling the cold." Daniel raised his eyebrows. "Do you want me to go get them?"

"They've gone ahead," Eric said, his back to the fire now. Glen was surprised how much cooler it felt with the two men blocking the heat. The temperature must really have dropped.

"We sent Tim ahead with a couple of the small teens and Marta to keep an eye on them. They should be in town by now," Jonno explained.

"Which means we really should get a move on. We don't want our surprise to be ruined." Eric rummaged in a messenger bag slung across his chest, pulling out a dog collar and a leash. He buckled the collar on his own neck, and hooked the leash onto it, tucking the loose end into his pocket.

"I'll be in charge of this until we get closer to the town," he said. "I don't want to tempt you."

Glen grinned, this was part of the plan. It was going to look as though he'd brought Eric to Terror. Eric would have his hands fastened behind his back with breakaway ties. Once they'd gained entrance to the town, Eric and Glen would overpower Terror. Then Jonno and the rest would take out the other former military men.

Glen and Daniel pulled on their gear. Daniel tossed Glen a pair of warm gloves, which he put on.

Outside, Eric sent the others on their way, leaving only the small group of men and women who would accompany Eric and Glen. Once everyone was gone, Eric and Glen stood in the circle of their team members, and Eric said, "Okay Glen, hit me."

Glen pulled his arm back and punched Eric square in the jaw.

Eric rocked back but stayed on his feet. "No blood," he said and grinned. "You're going to have to hit me harder than that."

The instinct to protect his hands was so ingrained in the surgeon that he had to collect himself. He wasn't a brain surgeon anymore, and a little damage to his hands wasn't going to matter. This time he got Eric square on the nose with an uppercut.

Eric grinned as his nose began bleeding. "Better," he said. "One more time for good measure. Give me a black eye."

This time Glen used a one-two punch, giving Eric a shiner. He watched as Eric's eye began swelling. "Shoot, I don't want you to be blind in that eye," he said. "I hit you too hard."

"Nah, I'll be fine," Eric said, touching his swollen eyelid.

"If it gets too bad, I'll have Ellen over there slice it to reduce the swelling. No worries." He knelt down and rubbed dirt all over his face and hands, then he straightened and dirtied Glen's face as well, making it look as though they'd been rolling in the dirt. "That's good," he said. "Showtime."

He led the way away from the cabin, Glen and the others falling into step behind him. They walked single file, silent and alert until they reached the road. Then they handcuffed Eric's hands behind his back with the breakaway cuffs. Glen took the end of the leash and "led" Eric down the middle of the road, the others ranging around them.

When they came close to being visible by the townspeople, Glen began yanking on the leash as Eric resisted. The others jeered at Eric, pushing him forward roughly and occasionally administering a punch or a kick in the butt. They were careful not to inflict actual damage, but Glen thought it looked pretty convincing as they marched up to the gate.

"Who's there?" called a voice from the other side of the wall.

"Glen Carter," Glen called back, "I've got a gift for Terror."

"What gift is that?" was the response.

"Take a look," Glen said, stopping about ten feet from the wall, dragging Eric with him. "I've got the resistance leader."

A man's head came around the gap in the wall, and a flashlight beam racked the group. Murmured voices came from the other side of the fence, and then some arguing.

"I can take him away again if you don't want him," Glen called out, putting as much sarcasm into his voice as he dared.

"Stay there," came the reply, "we're going to get the boss."

So they stayed, standing quietly, although Glen thought that to be convincing, Eric should be trying to get away. But as far as they could tell, there was no one on the other side of the wall watching. So, why should they waste their energy?

Glen had half a mind to take a look through the gap and see if anyone had been left behind. But the plan relied on this playing out a certain way, so he stayed put and tried to calm his impatience. He was here, and ready to make things happen, but the waiting irritated him. He was afraid they would get distracted from the task at hand.

It was twenty minutes before the sentries returned with Terror. Glen was pacing and just barely keeping his anger in check. When Terror stepped out through the gap in the wall, bringing Angelica with him, Glen let his anger show on his face. Once again the flashlight raked Glen's group, showing Eric standing dejected, his head down.

"Well, well," Terror said, "what did you bring me?" He circled Glen and Eric. "You know, of course, that you've got the heart of the resistance at the end of that rope?"

"I do," Glen said. "I wanted to prove to you that I wasn't one of them, didn't infiltrate your group as a spy. I want to live under your protection, and I brought you Eric as a gesture of good faith." He jerked Eric forward and handed the leash to Terror.

This was the cue and, of course, several things happened at once. Terror started to yanked on the leash, probably hoping Eric would faceplant at his feet, but Eric snapped out of the breakaway cuffs and lunged forward, grabbing the leash with one hand and snatching the knife from Terror's belt with the other. The guards, realizing that something was amiss, ran ahead to protect their leader, but not before Eric had sliced Terror's belly with the knife.

Gunfire flared from the top of the wall, but Tim must have succeeded in alerting the right people. Shots rang out from farther back in the town and the gunfire from the wall stopped abruptly. Glen knew that would be short-lived.

Others would take a stand on the wall, but perhaps his allies inside would thin their numbers.

Angelica was kneeling next to Terror, who was swearing and telling her he'd be fine. "Go find that drunk of a doctor," he said. "Tell him to bring dressings. It's only a flesh wound, but it's bleeding like a son of a bitch."

"I'm not leaving you to be finished off by one of these jackals," she hissed. She grabbed one of Terror's men, "Bring the doctor!" she yelled. "And you'll get him here in a hurry if you don't want your balls cut off."

Glen wouldn't put it past her to do that. The second wave of settlers opened fire on the wall the minute more guns appeared, and Glen stayed low to avoid being caught in the crossfire. He needed to get inside, but he would have to join the fray to make it there. Eric was trying to avoid being pummeled by a couple of men Glen recognized. What was it that Mia had called them? Third Eye and Boss Man, one had an eye tattooed on his forehead, and the other gave the orders. Well, he wasn't THE boss man, that would be Terror, but that's what Mia had called him.

Glen moved as quietly as he could, given the circumstances. He sucker punched Third Eye in the kidney, then delivered a knockout punch to his temple. Third Eye rolled on the ground, groaning, leaving Eric and Glen free to take down Boss Man. Glen double-checked they were down for the count by raising an eyelid on each of them.

"They'll be out for a while," he told Eric, "and probably won't be able to stand up straight for a day or two."

"Good," Eric said, taking off the collar and rubbing his neck. It was red and sore. "Those two jerk you around by the leash?" Glen asked.

Eric nodded, still rubbing his neck.

"Sorry," Glen said. "I should have made the collar breakaway too. That looks painful."

"I'll be okay," Eric said, "but look out behind you."

Glen turned to see another of Terror's henchmen bearing down on him. Glen kicked the man's knee. He folded into a heap on the ground, and Glen pistol-whipped him. The man didn't move, and Glen moved on.

Angelica was standing over Terror, teeth bared, looking like a cornered wolverine. She alternately was punching with her right hand and swiping a knife with her left. The attacking man was at least a foot taller and had the reach to match. But she was fierce and determined, and her adversary dropped back to keep from being gutted.

Glen thought her instinct would be to go after him, but she stayed put, straddling Terror, her knees bent, her eyes swiveling back and forth, searching for the next threat. Glen stayed well away. It might be Terror's day to die, but it wasn't Glen's day to kill him. He'd didn't like that he had a death on his conscience, and he didn't intend to add another.

One of Eric's men, an older man, might have been John, was struggling to pull a younger man from the wall. The younger man had his forearm around John's neck, trying to maintain a choke hold. Meanwhile, John had the front of the younger man's jacket, trying to dislodge him from his firing position, while the man held him tight against the wall.

Glen ran to him and grabbed the younger man's neck and shoulders, adding his weight to John's. Between the two of them, they dragged the younger man over the wall onto the ground. Glen grabbed the weapon that had fallen with him and checked to see if it was loaded.

"Don't shoot him!" John threw his body across that of the man on the ground, protecting him.

"I wasn't going to," Glen said, startled. "I was unloading the gun."

"He's my grandson," John said. "I had to get him off the wall before he got shot. We have to get him out of here."

"No, Grandad," John's grandson sputtered. "I have to fight, or he will kill Molly and the kids."

"Then we'll make it look good," Glen said. "Pretend to lose consciousness."

He turned the weapon and made a show of smacking the man on the head, but actually struck the dirt. The man went still. Glen went to drag him out of the range of fire, but John stopped him.

"We have to do this right," he muttered, "so there is no question he was in the fight." He took the gun from Glen and landed a blow on his grandson's face. Glen was startled, appalled that John would injure his kin so severely.

John looked at him and raised an eyebrow. "If this campaign doesn't end the way we want it to, I want there to be no doubt that Johnny here did his part." He shook his head. "I couldn't live with myself if anything happened to Molly or the children because I saved my namesake." He gestured to the man on the ground. "He's going to hurt like hell when he wakes up, but at least he'll be alive."

Glen put his hand on John's shoulder. "Are you okay now?" he asked.

John nodded. "I'm good to go, son. Go find those kids. Sounds like they need you."

Glen nodded and offered his hand to John to shake. "It's been my privilege, John," he said. "I hope we meet again under better circumstances."

John shook his hand and held it a moment. "Take care of yourself, Doc. We might need you again one day."

"And you." Glen released the man's hand and turned, heading straight for the gap in the wall. He figured he had a three-minute window before someone else came to fill the gap left by John's grandson, and he was going to take it.

He ran low, hunched over so that no one on the far side of the wall would be able to spot him. Hopefully, any of Eric's people would recognize him and refrain from shooting. He was not ready to die. "Not my day to die," he muttered under his breath. He ducked through the gateway and punched a startled youth in the nose. The boy went down. Glen stepped over him, and took a right, skirting back along the wall, staying low so as not to get shot by his own people.

CHAPTER EIGHTEEN

BY THE TIME the door to the basement opened Sally had bounded to her cell in two strides and clambered over the top of the wall. She landed hard on the other side. Mia could see the tears in her friend's eyes as she lay on the hard floor clutching her knee. By the time the boots were visible on the stairs, she was sitting up with her back against the bars, and Mia doubted anyone who didn't know Sally would know anything was wrong.

By the time the black-haired woman in army fatigues had made it to the bottom of the stairs and was staring at the light switch, Sally's color had returned to normal, and Mia thought they might actually get away with it. Meanwhile, Christian had moved to the back of his cell, where he could see in the shadows behind the stairs.

Mia appreciated that he was taking advantage of the few moments they would be able to see because she had no doubt this woman was going to turn off the light again. And if they switched them back on, she would have no doubt that one of the three could get out of their cell, and their next place of confinement would be even worse than this one. Probably tethered to a wall somewhere with chains around their necks.

"Why is this light on?" the woman asked.

"Because the guy who brought us down here left it on," Christian said. "Possibly so we could see to aim in our toilet hole."

She looked at him grimly, her mouth in a straight line and her eyes glinting. "I very much doubt that," she said. "Anthony is not soft-hearted. He wouldn't care if he was leaving little girls in the dark." She spoke the last sentence in a high singsong, mocking them.

"Well then, maybe he just forgot to turn it off," Mia said. "Maybe you should reprimand him." But she hoped the woman wouldn't. She had the distinct feeling that he, Anthony, was trying to help them. She made a mental note of his name, in case they ever saw him again.

"We don't leave lights on by mistake," the woman said. "Every person in this town knows how rare our electricity is. We don't waste it, and people in cells with nothing to do but sit around don't need lights." She snapped the lights off and stomped back up the stairs, leaving Mia and the others back in the dark.

"Christian?" Mia called across the room.

"Shush," he said. "Wait."

They waited, listening until they heard the faint sound of footsteps retreating from the door. She was trying to be quiet, sneaking so they couldn't tell she was gone, Mia thought.

"Wait," Christian said again.

Mia settled down, with her back against the concrete wall, which she thought was more comfortable than the bars. She started to count in her head, wanting to know how long Christian was going to make them wait. One, two, three...

Mia lost track around six hundred and twenty-five, the numbers jumbling around in her head. She began singing " Frère Jacques" out loud, and then "Allouette," remembering them from high school French. Those days seemed at once long ago and just yesterday. Here in the dark, she could see the classrooms and her fellow students, remembering the elation and despair. If she only had known what was coming, she wouldn't have bothered with the darker emotions, or at least she wouldn't have let what other students said affect her. Life was too short.

"Mia?" Christian spoke some time later, and she came out of the half-trance that she'd sunken into. "Sally?"

"I'm here," Sally said.

"Are you hurt?" Mia asked. "Will you be able to walk?"

"I'm okay," she said. "It just hurt when I landed."

"Did you see anything, Christian?" Mia asked.

"Yeah. Back behind the stairs, I think there is a bulkhead. Do you want to try turning the light on again, Sally?" he asked.

Mia could hear that Sally already was swarming up the bars of her cell. Up and over she went.

"I'm not going to turn on the light yet," her disembodied voice echoed in the dark. "I'm going to make my way over behind the stairs and see what I can find out with my fingers. Maybe I can open the bulkhead without the light. Why attract attention if we don't need to do so?

She shuffled past the stairs quietly, Mia could only just hear the rustling of her clothing. There were some soft scraping noises, but no chinks appeared, no tiny triangles of light. "Sally?" Mia called out quietly. "Any luck?"

"I think there is a door here. I just can't figure out how to open it," Sally said. "I'm trying to use my fingers, but my mind isn't cooperating." She sounded frustrated.

"Then why not try the light again?" Christian asked. "What's the worst that could happen?"

"That I'll see the light and catch you," Light flooded the basement, and the woman with the black hair was standing at the bottom of the stairs. Mia looked at the woman's feet. She still was in her army boots, but she was able to make it down the stairs unheard. Now that was a feat, and Mia felt a grudging respect for the woman's abilities.

"I did tell you what happens next, didn't I?" It wasn't so much a question as a statement. And it was true, she had told them that the next place they would be held would be worse.

"Sally," Mia cried out, "run!"

The woman headed around the back of the stairs, and Sally popped out from the other direction. She ran up the stairs, and Mia heard an "Oof!" And then Sally came back down, propelled by the man who Mia thought of as "the thug," but whose name was apparently Anthony.

He looked grim as he guided Sally back to her cell and handcuffed her to the bars. He relocked the door as the woman came back from the dark end of the basement.

"Any problems back there, Angelica?" he asked.

"No. There wasn't much that girl was going to see in the dark," Angelica said. "Are the other two secure?"

"Yes. There's no space for either of those two to go over the top," Anthony said. "And this one," he pointed at Sally, "is hobbled."

"I still think we should put them in the hole," Angelica said.

"That's a little extreme, don't you think? The three of them are just kids, really. And they haven't hurt anyone." Anthony smiled and put an arm on her shoulder.

"Tell that to Weston," she said, and pointed at Mia. "That one dropped a set of tires on his head."

"Weston is tough," Anthony said. "He'll live. The hole is a

pit, and it's hard to feed and water people there. I don't think we need to starve them, do you? They only were trying to find their friend." He led her upstairs, and Mia was surprised that Angelica let him influence her. The two of them turned out the light as they went by, which was unfortunate, but at least they weren't in the hole, whatever that was.

Glen left the battle and slipped down a side street, away from the gunfire and shouting. He was headed for the area around the library, going the long way around the perimeter rather than through town. The road less traveled seemed like the best option.

He had to stop and hide more often than he would have liked. There were a lot of people out patrolling the wall. Finally, he moved a couple of blocks toward the center of town so he could avoid them. He planned to go straight to the library, since that was the center of Terror's operation. They wouldn't go to the trouble of holding hostages far from there.

At least he wouldn't if he were in charge.

But as he moved quickly along he recognized the street where he'd been kept in the closet. He thought a second and decided that, while it wasn't likely they all were stuffed into one closet, it wouldn't hurt to check it out just in case. Rather than have to come back later. So, he took a detour and headed for what he thought of as Angelica's house. He didn't know for sure it was hers, but she acted like she owned it.

He wondered where she was. Most probably not at home. Still, he'd have to be careful not to scare the children he'd heard when he'd been there before. He only wanted to be sure his three charges weren't there before he moved on.

The street was quiet, but he wondered if people were watching him from behind their curtains. Most of the houses had a disused look to them, and he speculated that most of them were empty. Maybe this wasn't a thriving town after all.

When he reached the house, he went quickly up the steps and tried the door. It was open, and he wasn't surprised. What need was there to lock your home when you lived in a walled town? He slipped inside and up the stairs to the room where he'd been held. He listened at the closet door. No sound.

He cracked open the door, preparing to take a look inside, when the door slammed into him, smacking his face and bruising his eye. He was knocked back onto the floor, and when he looked up, he found himself looking into the face of a teenage boy.

"Who are you?" the boy asked.

"Glen," he said, still a little dazed. "Who are you?"

"Zeke. What are you doing in our house?" the boy said, looking confused.

"Looking for some friends of mine," Glen said, sitting up. "Have you seen two young women and a man? College-aged, you know, in their early twenties."

"I heard that some kids were found in town," Zeke said. "They hunted them down at the tire shop and took them away."

"Know where they took them?" Glen got up gingerly from the floor, weary of the boy, although he didn't seem inclined to throw Glen down again.

"No, they don't tell us important things like that. I only know about the three people because I was listening from the top of the stairs when my mom was talking about it. But probably somewhere at the other end of town. All the families are at the south end. They won't let us go up to the north end of town. We aren't allowed to go anywhere near the school or the library."

"I've got to go," Glen said, but then had another thought. "What were you doing in the closet?" he asked.

"My mom didn't want me to join the fighting, so she asked

Angelica to lock me up. She put me in that closet, and I've been waiting for my chance to break out. I'm sorry about your eye." Zeke looked a little sheepish. "I don't really want to fight. I just want to see my dad. He was a firefighter, and they ran him out of town. I miss him."

"Yeah, well, you should stay away from the fighting. You could get shot. Stay in the house. When the fighting is all over, go look for your dad. He'll be wanting to see you too." Glen hoped the man still would be alive.

"How do you know?" Zeke asked.

"Because I just came from the settlement and all those men miss their families. How could they not? So, will you stay away, or do I have to lock you back in the closet?" Glen asked.

"No, I'll stay here. I'll go up to the attic and see if I can spot him from there. My mom would kill me if I got shot." He seemed unaware of the irony in his statement.

Glen nodded and left the house. He hoped the boy would do as he said and stay away from the battle. But Glen also knew that, at that age, he would have agreed with anything an adult said to their face, and then gone and done whatever he'd wanted to do in the first place.

Back out on the street, Glen turned away from the center of town and headed down one of the lesser used streets, heading toward the north end of town and the library. After what Zeke had said, he was sure the three were being held in the vicinity of the library.

He ran now, not in a panic, but with a sense of urgency. The battle was in full swing, gunfire coming from both sides of the wall, and he was worried someone might get the bright idea to use the three as bait or in some sort of hostage negotiation.

He saw some people coming down one of the cross streets, and they shouted to or at him. He couldn't tell which.

He waved and kept running, hoping they would mistake him for one of their own, whichever side they were on. That was one of the problems with this fight, he thought, you couldn't tell who was who. They all looked the same.

He cut across the playground of the elementary school and headed straight for the back door of the library. He went in slowly. This wasn't the emergency door Mia had used when they had been held here, but the back entrance into the big hall that ran the length of the building from front to back, splitting the ground floor in two.

The place seemed deserted, but he slid behind one of the columns and listened for a while. If there was anyone left in this building, they weren't making any noise. He snuck down the staircase to the basement, which appeared to consist of workrooms and meeting spaces. His charges were nowhere to be seen. He headed back up the stairs. He searched the rest of the building, floor by floor, finding only one person, an elderly man bent over some very antique looking maps, who didn't appear to see or hear Glen. Unless there was a hidden attic, the kids were not in this building.

He headed next door to where he had bandaged Terror's hand. Here he wasn't so lucky, a glance through the back door window revealed a man sitting at the kitchen table, cleaning his gun. Glen was about to turn away and try the front when he realized he'd seen this man at the settlement. He was one of Eric's men.

Glen tapped gently on the window. The man's response was immediate. He was up and out of his chair in a heartbeat, another firearm in his hand. Glen raised both his hands to show he didn't have a weapon at the ready, and the man seemed to recognize him. The man put his gun down and smiled. Then he put a finger to his lips and came over to the door, opening it carefully.

"I'm not alone," he breathed. "There are others in the

next room, but I believe I have what you are looking for," and gestured for Glen to enter.

Glen stepped through the doorway and followed Eric's man into the kitchen when there was an unholy crash from beneath their feet. Before he knew it, Glen had been shoved into a broom closet, and the door slammed shut.

CHAPTER NINETEEN

IN THE BASEMENT Mia was pressed against the front of her cell, trying to figure out what was going on. Sally had been muttering, and Mia could hear the sound of metal sliding over metal, which she thought must be the end of one of the handcuffs that was wrapped around the cell's bar. Then there had been an "Oomph!" a cry of pain and a cacophony of sound that sounded like nothing Mia ever had heard before. It was loud, hurt her ears, and if she didn't know better, she'd have said that the block of cells on the other side of the room had collapsed.

"Sally?" she yelled. She wanted to ask if she was alright, but that was stupid. None of those noises indicated anything was alright. "Christian? Do you know what happened?"

"Not sure." He sounded shaken. "Give me a minute."

The sound of running feet came from upstairs. Lots of feet, some traveling across the length of the house, others thumping down the stairs from the upper floors. The basement door banged open, more feet coming down those steps, and then the light came on.

It took Mia a minute, the light hurt her eyes, but when

she could focus she saw an unholy mess on the other side of
the basement and a group of people standing at the bottom
of the basement stairs, gaping. Sally laid white-faced under
what once was the front of her cell. The arm that still was
handcuffed to the cell bar was twisted, and at such a strange
angle Mia knew it must be broken.

Sally was panting and conscious, cut, bruised and swearing, which Mia took as a good sign. But the look of that arm
made her a little woozy, and she looked away, catching the eye
of Anthony, the thug. He looked grim, but there was something else in his expression, something Mia couldn't read.
Strangely, it gave her hope. He gave her a nod so small that
she almost thought she imagined it. Then he joined the
others trying to free Sally.

He knelt down, straddling one of the bars, and unlocked
the handcuff from her wrist, leaving the other end attached
to the cage. He stood and stepped away from the metal.
Three of the others lifted the front of the cell up and away
from her, holding it until Anthony and a woman in fatigues
and a T-shirt gently moved Sally out from underneath. Then
Anthony lifted Sally in his arms and carried her away, up the
stairs.

As they went, Sally held out her uninjured hand and piti-
fully called Mia's name.

"I'll come as soon as I can, Sal," she said, reaching her arm
through the bars as if to hold Sally's hand.

Then Sally was gone.

The four of Terror's crew who were left in the basement
were working on repairing the cell Sally had destroyed. Mia
wondered how Sally had gotten over the first two times
without a problem but figured the handcuff must have
thrown off her balance. Now that she thought about it, how
did Sally expect to get over? The ring of the metal bracelet
would have been stuck at the top of the cage once her body

went over the other side. Sally would have been left standing tiptoe, her arm straight in the air if the whole thing hadn't collapsed on her.

Mia glimpsed Christian leaning against the far side of his cell watching her. He looked tired, but caught her glance, and winked at her with the eye away from the others. Then he glanced into the shadows and tilted his head in that direction. Could he see something back there that she couldn't? A way out?

They'd have to wait until Sally got back, which could be a while. She didn't know if it was day or night outside, or how long it would take for the doctor to come. The sound of gunfire in the distance had reached them a while back. There could be injuries that the doctor would have to take care of before he could come look at Sally. It could be a while.

She sat and watched Terror's people bolting the front of Sally's cell back into place. One of the men went inside to check that the back still was firmly attached to the wall. He tugged, and the side away from Christian's cell came away from the wall. The string of expletives that filled the basement made Mia smile. Sally had done a number on that cell. It was karmic justice.

Glen was at the point of cracking open the broom closet's door when he heard footsteps on the stairs from the basement. Damn it! He'd left it too long. Would he be stuck in here forever? He knew he was being dramatic, but straddling a vacuum cleaner, with a broom on one side and a duster in his face on the other, was slightly unmanly. He was just another item shoved in the closet.

The steps stopped outside his hiding place, and he held his breath.

"I'm going to open this door, and you are going to see something that will surprise you." It was Anthony on the other side of the door. "No matter what you see, you need to remain quiet, okay?"

"Okay," he whispered and thought he heard an echo on the other side of the door.

The door opened, and Anthony stood there holding Sally, her left arm hanging oddly. Her eyes opened wide when she saw Glen, and she burst into tears. Noiseless tears, thankfully.

"Come on, we can't be found here." Anthony turned and led Glen to the front of the house, and then up the stairs and along the hall to a room at the back. He nudged the door open with his foot and carried Sally in and placed her on the bed.

"You have to be quiet," Anthony said. "I'll tell the others that I sent someone to get the doctor, and I'll bring up the first aid kit, but we don't have anything to set that arm with."

"I don't think it's broken," Glen said, "just dislocated. I think I can manipulate it back into place and use a pillowcase and some strips of fabric as a sling to hold it in place while it heals. Unless you've got an elastic bandage around here someplace?"

"I'll look." Anthony glanced toward the door. "But I think you have to assume that you need to make do with what's in this room. I've got to go. If you hear anyone coming down the hall, Glen, you probably should hide in the closet."

"Again with the closet." Glen shook his head. "What is it with this town and closets?"

Anthony laughed softly. "What is it with you and closets? I'll try and stop back in."

When Anthony left the room, Glen turned to Sally. He sat on the bed next to her and spoke softly.

"Your arm is dislocated, Sally, and it's going to hurt when I put it back in place." He wiped the sheen of sweat off her upper lip.

"It hurts now," she said, licking her lips. "Pretty badly."

"It's going to hurt worse, but then it will subside to an ache. At least that's what I'm told. I've never dislocated my shoulder." He took hold of her upper arm and her shoulder.

"But you've done this before? Haven't you?" she asked, her eyes wide. "Put a shoulder back in place?"

"Yes. I have done this before." What he didn't say was that it was when he was a medical student. Neurosurgeons did not spend much time popping dislocated joints back into place. He placed a hand on her shoulder to keep her steady and felt the joint. She had her teeth gritted but didn't make a sound.

"Okay," he said, trying to keep his voice casual, "toss the pillows on the floor and lie down on the far side of the bed."

She did as she was told, but she didn't look happy about it. Glen slipped off his shoes and sat cross-legged on the other side of the mattress. He slid one stockinged foot in her armpit, took the limp arm and gently pulled. The noise she was making wasn't loud in the slightest, but it left no doubt in Glen's mind that she was in a lot of distress. However, there was no stopping now. He continued pulling the arm straight away from her body, using his foot to keep the rest of her from shifting.

It was field medicine at its worst. He wasn't trained for it, had a sketchy idea of how it was done at best, and it was only his knowledge of human anatomy that made it possible at all. It took much longer than he would have liked, gently rotating her arm while stretching the arm bone away from the socket but, finally, it slipped back in.

Sally stopped groaning and opened her eyes. Glen gave her a thumbs-up and wiped the sweat from his face with his sleeve. Anthony hadn't come back with the first aid kit, so Glen got his shoes back on and went to the door. There wasn't any noise from this floor or the one below. So, he went in search of a linen closet or bathroom, somewhere he could find what he needed. The bathroom turned out to be right across the hall, but there wasn't anything in the drawers or behind the mirror that could immobilize her arm.

There was a bottle of painkillers, however, and he pocketed it before slipping back out into the hall. He finally found a linen closet and pulled a sheet that looked like it had been around since the dawn of time. That was perfect for his purposes, since he needed to tear it.

Sally was sitting up examining her shoulder when he came back in the room. She had movement but grimaced with pain.

"It's going to hurt for a few days, maybe a week," Glen said quietly. "But it will be okay. I'm going to put it in a sling and then wrap it close to your body. It will hurt less if you can't move it."

He set out ripping the sheet with his teeth and then shredding it with his hands. A triangular piece worked well for a sling, which he slid behind Sally's neck and then tied in front of her body so the knot wouldn't be uncomfortable. Then he took longer strips and wrapped them snuggly, securing her arm to her body.

"I'm as certain as I can be that your shoulder will heal nicely. We don't have access to X-rays, so I'm not one hundred percent. I'd advise you to see your primary care provider, except those don't exist anymore. It's all field medicine." He smiled at her. "You'll be okay."

He sat down on the hope chest. He leaned his head back against the wall and closed his eyes. How long had it been since he'd slept? Would Sally take it amiss if he lied down on the bed next to her? Just to sleep. He felt himself drifting. Never mind, he thought, I can sleep right here.

"Glen!" The urgency in her voice cut through the haze in his mind, and he started awake, even though she hadn't spoken loudly.

"Sorry," he said. "It's been a while since I slept. Are you in pain? I grabbed these for you." He fumbled in his pocket and brought out the plastic container of over-the-counter painkillers.

"Later," she said, "when I have some water. Right now we need to figure out how to get Mia and Christian out of the basement."

"What was that ruckus in the basement?" he asked. "Were you breaking out?"

"Something like that." She rubbed the wrist that had been cuffed. It had hurt when her full weight had rested there, hanging from the bars. At least for the second before her shoulder had given way. And then the front of the cell had fallen on her, and that hurt almost as much as her shoulder.

"I was trying to get us out of here," she said, shifting on the bed. "Those cells downstairs are brutal. All concrete and metal and they left us in the pitch dark." She glanced out the window. "Look, the dawn is coming."

Glen followed her gaze. Sure enough, there was a faint light in the sky to the east, above the ridge. Would the light help them or hinder them?

"Tell me about the cells in the basement," he said. "Will we be able to get them out?"

"We'll need to steal the key from Anthony," she said, and then frowned. "Wait. Did he just help us? He brought you up here to help me."

Glen didn't want to tell her too much in case her face gave Anthony away at a crucial moment. There still was gunfire echoing out there, and Anthony would need his cover until it was all over. "He may be sympathetic to us," Glen said. "I might be able to convince him to lend us the keys."

Sally got up from the bed. "Let's go then. What are we waiting for?"

"When you created all that noise earlier, I counted at least seven pairs of footsteps responding. None of those people have yet to come back out of the basement. I'm all for running in, guns blazing." He stopped speaking.

She was frowning and shaking her head. "That's not true. You are very cautious. You want to wait until the townies are finished down there."

"I don't like the odds," he admitted. "Especially when all we have to do is wait them out."

"But Mia and Christian don't know you're alive," she said. "And they don't know what happened to me."

"They are safe. And the lights probably are on if they are repairing your cell." He thought a moment. "How many cells are down there?"

"Eight, or maybe ten," she said, a furrow between her brows. "When the lights were on I was focused on the other end of the basement. I think there is a way out over there."

"I wonder why they are so focused on making sure all the cells are functioning?" he asked. "Maybe Terror inspects them. He might insist they remain in working order."

"Or maybe they are down there torturing Mia and Christian," she gasped. "We should at least go listen at the door." She was up and at the door before he could speak.

He got up and drew her gently away from the door, bringing her back to the bed.

"I'll go listen at the door," he said. "But I can't think of any reason they would want to torture any of you. There's no information to be obtained."

"But maybe they're using it as a way to keep me in line," Sally said, her eyes wide.

"Look at yourself. You won't be doing any climbing for a very long time. There is no need to torture Mia and Christian. But stay here, and I will see what I can find out. Okay? You'll stay put?"

She nodded, and he headed out the door.

CHAPTER TWENTY

GLEN PAUSED at the bottom of the staircase, listening. All the sounds still were coming from the basement. He slipped silently into the kitchen, walking along the wall in hope the boards wouldn't creak.

Anthony was in the kitchen, sitting at the table. He put his finger to his lips, got up and led Glen out of the kitchen and around the house to stand near the street. The street lights were not lit, that would have been a waste of power, and there was no moon. The faint light in the sky did not affect the town as of yet, so the two men barely could see each other's faces.

"Sally is worried they are torturing Christian and Mia," Glen said. "She sent me to check."

Anthony snorted. "Like we have time for torturing children. Terror is expecting an influx of captives this evening. He wants all the cells operable. So my crew is down there repairing the damage that girl did. They also will check all the others. Is she okay? The girl who broke the bars?"

"She'll be fine," Glen said. "It will hurt for a while, but she'll heal."

"Brave one, that," Anthony said darkly. "She is not easily subdued. She should learn when to wait."

"They are young," Glen replied. "Barely into their twenties. They haven't learned the value of patience." He rubbed his chin. "I'm not feeling too patient myself. I want to get them out of here before anything else happens. Can you help us get away from here?"

"Not without blowing my cover," Anthony said. "But I'll give you the means to escape. I have a spare key that works to open both the cells and the bulkhead in the basement. I will make sure I have an alibi so I won't get blamed."

Glen felt Anthony press something into his hand. It was warm from Anthony's pocket, and Glen slipped it into his.

"I will go get the girl and bring her to you," Anthony said. "Listen at the bulkhead door. When the others leave the basement, the light will go out. You'll be able to see that. The door is not tight. Go in, release your friends and run to the end of the road, north. There is an exit there. Don't fall into the ditch. Skirt the wall, staying close until you see the path into the woods on the east. From there it is up to you. We're running out of time. I will get the girl. You stay here."

He faded away, almost silently. Glen stayed where he was, and in less than five minutes the front door opened, and Sally came down the steps. She hesitated, looking left and right.

"I'm here," Glen breathed, realizing she couldn't see him after the bright light inside the house.

He took her hand, leading her around the house to the bulkhead. The light still was on in the basement, and they could hear the others talking. They were complaining about the people who had done such a shoddy job installing the cells. Not long after, the sounds of boots on the stairs reached them and then the light went out.

Glen reached for the key, but Sally put a hand out to

restrain him. "The light switch is at the bottom of the stairs," she said. "Give them a minute to clear the area."

They stood, Glen counting to a hundred in his mind before producing the key and opening the lock. It turned without a sound, which Glen found interesting. Someone had wanted to be sure the door could be unlocked without attracting attention. He pulled up the door and peered down into the dark hole. Sally knelt and produced a flashlight from the floor, then shined it downward. There was a ladder attached to the concrete wall that lined the bulkhead.

"You'll have to stay here," Glen said. "Try to stay out of sight."

She nodded and handed him the flashlight. He handed it back.

"Shine it into the hole for me, will you? I need my hands to navigate the ladder. And then if anyone approaches, you shine it in their eyes and run." He waited for her to nod again before letting himself down the ladder.

She kept the light low and pointed into the basement so he could see the glint of light on the bars down into the basement. It took him only minutes to release Christian and Mia, relock the cells, and usher them up the bulkhead ladder. At the top, he re-locked the door and hid the key under the protruding metal edge. Not one of them had said a word.

They ran around the house and out onto the street, turning north toward the closest gate. But before they'd even passed the library, a group of people rounded the corner, coming toward them. Terror was leading them, his hand holding a blood-soaked rag against the wound in his belly.

Glen tried to stop their forward momentum, to get his group out of sight, but it was too late, and the daylight was becoming too bright. If he could see the rag in Terror's hand, then the four of them must be visible as well. The two groups approached each other, stopping a good fifteen feet apart.

Terror walked into the space between the groups and Glen followed suit. They met, three feet apart, and glowered at each other as the sky lightened in the east. Glen could see now that Terror's face was white with pain, and there was a crazy restlessness in his eyes. He would have to stay alert if he was going to stay alive.

"You should not have come back," Terror said. "I will kill all four of you now."

"Why kill us, Tyrell? Uh, Terror?" Glen quickly corrected his mistake. He didn't want to antagonize this man. "We are no threat to you. I just want to take my friends somewhere safe. Somewhere away from here. We'll never come to this town again."

"You're right. You won't. Dead people don't get to return." Terror laughed, and there were a few faint-hearted twitters behind them.

It wouldn't be long before more of Terror's men would arrive, Glen thought. He might be able to get them past this group of tired and bleeding townspeople, but when Terror's henchmen came, it would be a lot more difficult. They probably wouldn't escape without injury.

Angelica pushed through from the back of the crowd and joined Terror, facing Glen. She stood close to his side and spoke quietly into his ear. Glen couldn't hear what she had to say, but he doubted it was in their favor. Likely it was something to do with her getting to kill him because he'd come back to the town. Terror grinned and licked his lips.

"How about hand-to-hand combat with my general here?" he asked, licking his lips in anticipation.

"That would be very satisfying, don't you think? If you win, the four of you go free. If not..." he shrugged.

"You'll already be dead, so it won't matter to you what happens to them." He nodded his head in the direction of

Mia, Sally, and Christian. "But I'm sure we'll get some kind of enjoyment out of them."

"I'd rather fight you," Glen said with a sneer. "Not some mewling little girl. Where is the joy in that? Where is the triumph?" He tossed his head in the direction of his group. "Sally could fight Angelica. That might be a fair match."

Angelica laughed. "I could destroy that child before she even realized it had happened. And then I would kill you. I would slice you into little pieces until there was nothing left. Would you like to die like that? Piece by piece?" She fingered the knife in her belt.

Glen noticed two things that surprised him. While Terror and Angelica were threatening to kill them, the group behind them had started backing away. These were not the fierce warriors pledged to support Terror, but frightened towns-people who wanted nothing more than to go back into their homes and tend to their wounds.

The other thing he noticed was the girl he had tried to help, the one he suspected Terror had beaten and raped, had joined the group supporting him. Only, while the others backed slowly away, fading into the dawn, she was moving steadily forward.

"Christian!" Glen called. "Come here, quickly."

"Calling for backup?" Angelica mocked.

Christian approached warily, not understanding why Glen needed him.

"See that woman?" Glen said quietly, so Terror wouldn't hear and look to see her approach. "Stop her from joining us. I don't want her to get hurt." Well, not anymore hurt than she already was, but Christian didn't know about that.

"I'll try," Christian said and faded off to the side, relieved to be away from Terror again.

Glen hoped Christian could reach the woman before Terror noticed her, but Glen would have to keep their attention on himself. He didn't have a firearm anymore. He'd given the one Eric had lent him to Jonno, so he took the knife from his belt and tossed it on the ground.

"Which of you would like to go first?" Glen said, watching Christian approach the woman from the corner of his eye. "Terror? Are you up for a little Mano e Mano? Wear me down so your little girl can finish me?"

Angelica hissed, and Terror dropped his gun belt.

"With pleasure," Terror said. He threw a punch with a quickness that startled Glen, but he was able to dodge it just the same. The next one landed square on the side of Glen's head, but Glen was able to retaliate with a blow to Terror's injured gut. Glen realized it was the injury Eric had given him and became distracted, wondering what had happened to Eric.

"Let me help you," Angelica pleaded.

"No," Terror said. "I will take care of this. You can have the others after he is dead."

Terror landed two quick jabs to Glen's gut while he was trying to see where Christian and the woman were. The air whooshed out of him, and Glen decided he'd better pay attention to what Terror was doing. He noticed the wound in Terror's gut was leaking blood again and he aimed another punch at the spot. Terror quickly turned away, but Glen still heard his grunt of pain as the jab grazed him.

Terror lunged forward and grabbed Glen around the neck, squeezing. His eyes bulging with rage. Angelica laughed and moved toward Mia and Sally. Glen tried calling out to them, warning them to run, but his airway was collapsing under the pressure of Terror's grip. He tried punching and kneeing Terror, but their bodies were too close together, so his blows were ineffectual. The world was beginning to black around the edges.

Run! He tried to telegraph his words to the girls. He

couldn't see them, he couldn't yell to them. Run, run, run! His body was desperate for air, and he was losing consciousness when Terror's grip abruptly went slack. Glen fell to the ground, gasping for air. He thought Terror must be playing with him, giving him a minute before he finished him off.

But then Terror landed on the road next to Glen, his eyes no more than a foot away. What Glen saw there was surprise and shock, and then the life went out of them.

Glen looked up to see the woman, God he wished he could remember her name, who was holding a long thin stiletto knife, and it was covered in blood. She had taken her revenge on Terror. Glen rolled onto his back, panting and looking at the morning sky. Oh, how fitting it was that Terror had met his end at the hands of one of his victims. There really was poetic justice in the world.

A scream came from his left and, remembering the girls, he got up, frantically looking for what had become of them. But it wasn't Sally or Mia who were making the noise, it was Angelica. The girls had taken her down. Mia was sitting on her back with Christian helping her cuff Angelica with the new plastic handcuffs Angelica had kept in her belt. Meanwhile, Sally sat on her legs. They all were sweaty and dirty, but their faces showed nothing but elation.

It was then Mia looked over at him and burst into tears.

"What?" he asked. "What is it? We're all okay. We won."

"They told us you were dead," she sobbed. "They showed us your bloody shirt, and it had a hole in it, and it was soaked in blood."

"I'm still wearing my shirt," he said quietly, getting up to join her on Angelica's back. They sat side by side, and he put an arm around her shoulders. "They were winding you up, Mia. Really, look at me, I'm not nearly as dead as they claimed."

She laughed but then nodded toward the woman standing

over Terror's body. "What about her? Is she going to be okay?"

"I hope so," Glen said. "I'll see if she'll talk to me before we leave. And if there is a therapist in this town, I'll hook them up. But I think she may just have exorcised some demons. At least I hope so."

Not long afterward, Eric showed up and had Jonno and Anthony haul Angelica away. Eric joined Glen, Christian and the girls on the curb. Christian pried Mia from Glen, and they were whispering together and holding hands. Sally was talking to Jack, who had crawled through the drainage pipe. They were laughing together, and Glen had the impression the boy was telling Sally the story of his part in the battle.

Daniel, the man Glen had spent the evening with in the cottage in the woods, came up and held out a hand for Glen to shake.

"I guess neither of us will be taking on the responsibility of the other's family," Glen said. "For which I am grateful."

"Me as well," Daniel said. "I'm surprised and delighted. Will you come on occasion and share a meal with us? It would be our pleasure if you would."

"Of course." Glen smiled. "But I'll probably have to bring my motley crew with me."

"I insist they come," Daniel replied, grinning. "Wouldn't want such fine young people to go hungry."

"Why don't you stay with us in the town?" Eric interrupted. "We could use a good doctor."

"I'll stay until we get everyone treated," Glen said. "And I'll supervise your drunk doctor while I'm here – make sure he's up to snuff and off the stuff."

Eric laughed. "Yeah, he needs a little intervention. But, you know, he may be better now that Terror is gone. That man was enough to drive anyone to drink."

"Yeah, maybe," Glen said,

Eric hoped it was true.

"But after that, we are going back to my cabin. I'm not saying you can't call on my services if they are needed, but it's been a long time since I've lived near people, and these three," he nodded to his new family, "are going to be hard enough to get used to. But we'll come when you need us. I understand you all know where to find me?" He raised his eyebrows at Eric.

Eric grinned. "Yes, we have been spying on you. It's true. But only in a good way." He nodded over Glen's shoulder. "I think that Sally might be glad to stay on a little longer."

Glen looked over to see Sally talking with Anthony. He grinned to himself. He had a feeling they'd be getting regular visitors from the town.

———

FIND out what happens in part three! Available Now!

CPSIA information can be obtained
at www.ICGtesting.com
Printed in the USA
BVHW032120060120
568776BV00001B/86/P